WHISPERS

IN THE

WATERS

To the Author of my faith

CHAPTER 1

A proper lady has no secrets. She offers smiles to potential suitors, moves with effortless grace through crowded ballrooms and theaters, and charms all with her words. She conceals nothing society might find troubling, nothing the world might examine and condemn.

What I kept concealed meant I'd never qualify as a proper lady, but I'd always believed Aunt Caris to be the epitome of a gentlewoman—until the fateful morning the letter from Milburn arrived, hinting she held secrets of her own.

A quarter hour earlier, Ada and Ainslie had departed to pay a call on Aunt Melisina, and in the absence of my sisters, a hush settled over the house. In the blissful quiet, I sorted through one of the thick notebooks containing my sketches and records on various herbs, in hopes of finding the perfect addition to the salve I was attempting to formulate for Ainslie. She'd asked me to concoct a solution to remove the peculiar silvery-gray scar etched across her upper arm, one which had resisted all efforts to erase its existence so far. I enjoyed the puzzle of combining and recombining plants with various healing properties to find the ones best suited, despite the fact that something in the unusual symmetry of her scar appeared to me more appealing than distasteful.

Ainslie had claimed it was a small matter, "scarce worth a mention—only, do you think you might have something on hand to treat it?" Yet when she'd spoken, her lively features had stilled, and her usual smile had faded. No matter my opinion, the scar clearly troubled her, and that provided reason enough for its removal.

Sunlight poured through the wide windows of the morning room, refracting light from the fountain across the pages of my book and blurring the inked images. Never mind that no one had seen nisi this far from a Crossing in years; every home that could manage it still kept a fountain somewhere to appease the household fae, who preferred running water for their ablutions—or at least, so tradition held. If one could avoid enmity from the Otherkind, so much the better for one's health.

I shifted positions and rifled through several more pages before landing on an entry for briony, its tiny white flowers and dark leaves common enough in the hedges and byways, its root valued for cleansing the skin. Perhaps this would complement the others I planned to include in the salve, which held more soothing properties. I tapped the image, considering. This endeavor would be best accomplished in the gardens, where instinct could partner with analysis, but Aunt Caris preferred to stay in company, even if we exchanged no conversation, and I couldn't disappoint her.

Across from me, she penned the final lines of an invitation to the small dinner party she intended to hold in a fortnight. Her face creased in a smile as she stacked the completed invitation atop its companions. Even at rest, she looked radiant as a sunbloom, her coppery hair as striking as its richly-hued petals, her full figure sharing its soft curves.

She capped the bottle of ink and returned it to her small round worktable. "There, that's done. Unless you wished to invite anyone to the dinner, Jessa?"

I'd rather flee to the safety of Father's study for the evening than join the party, let alone add to its number. But I could never confess that to Aunt Caris. I placed a ribbon to mark my entry on briony and set the book aside. "No thank you, Aunt Caris. I'm certain you've already planned the guest list to perfection."

Though she didn't permit herself a full smile, her eyes crinkled at the corners as if she perceived that which I'd left unspoken. Whatever exhortation she might have offered, our butler Holden interrupted, arriving with the post. I welcomed the delivery since I hoped the morning post would bring an answer from Milton and Sons, the publisher I believed might be a good fit for my herbalism guide. Despite how often my expectations had been dashed, anticipation blossomed as constant and sweet as a carpet of violets in spring.

After Holden left, I sorted the letters—a lengthy missive from a fellow herbalist for me; two notes for Ada and three for Ainslie, more than likely from lovelorn suitors; and a letter for Aunt Caris, along with a large stack of invitations which would delight Ada and Ainslie alike.

But even a second, more thorough search failed to reveal a message from Milton and Sons. My spirits sank at the delay. Would they be one of many to decry my guide as too costly an undertaking, never mind the need it filled?

Aunt Caris glanced up, her green eyes bright. "Anything for me, my dear?"

"There are a number of invitations, but only one letter." I

offered her a small envelope with her name scrawled across the front. Its paper was the pale brown of a withered beech leaf—which was unusual, given that most ladies favored crisp, white pages for their correspondence, often perfumed and written in flourishing script.

Aunt Caris opened her letter and skimmed the contents. Then she crumpled it into the pocket of her gown and stood abruptly, her ever-blooming cheeks pale.

Unease pricked along my spine. "Did you receive bad news?"

"What?" She started and then clutched at her pocket as if it contained a burning ember. "No . . . of course not, dear, it's just a headache."

Aunt Caris did not possess the art of dissembling, and though she rubbed her temples, I distrusted her words.

"I believe I'll go rest for a bit," she said.

I rose as well, her disquiet wakening my own. "Shall I prepare some lavender tea? If I add willow bark, it might ease the pain."

"Yes, dear. That would be lovely, but there's no hurry." Despite her expression of gratitude, her voice remained abstracted, and she wandered from the morning room like one in a dream.

I watched her go, a knot forming in my stomach. Since Mother's passing fourteen years ago, Aunt Caris had provided continual love and care for us, looking after Ada, Ainslie, and me as if we were her blood daughters. She always overflowed with kindness, lively goodwill, and sometimes a propensity toward overmanagement of our affairs—but she'd certainly never succumbed to the vapors or indulged in unnecessary theatrics, no matter how trying the circumstances.

If something troubled her, it must be a situation worthy of concern, not a frivolous matter. The knot in my stomach tightened. I wanted to run after her and demand answers, but she clearly desired peace and privacy. Perhaps after an interval of solitude, she'd be more amenable to discussion. So instead I made my way to the glasshouse, which sheltered my more delicate plants from the chill that still crept into our early spring days.

As I wove through the garden, the plants pressed upon my awareness, like the pricking of a thorn into tender flesh. Their voices called to me—the bright, chirpy notes of the yellow-and-white hellebore bobbing along the path, the shy, whispered tones of the delicate lily of the valley, and the sap-sticky sweep of maple limbs bowing in the breeze.

No, I shouldn't listen, shouldn't hear such things. Normal people didn't, so neither would I. If Father found out these aberrations had returned, and indeed strengthened, he would be crushed. When I first experienced the whispers after Mother's passing, he'd done an admirable job of constructing an argument that they'd come as a result of her death. He believed they were my unconscious attempt to stay close to her by connecting with the stories of the Otherworld that she loved to share, an influence heightened in times of emotional stress. An influence that was essential to shut down lest word escape and scandal ensue—or worse, lead to accusations of fae-touch that would bring down the wrath of the Vigil and land me in an Institution. Since I was small, he had warned me to seek calm and lock untidy emotions away, to prevent this fault from overcoming me—which meant I couldn't allow the upset experienced by Aunt Caris to become my own. She would not wish it, not after all she and Father had done for me.

I entered the glasshouse, and the pressure increased as each living thing vied for my attention. A throbbing ache built at the nape of my neck.

Blight and rot, this would never do.

With a long-practiced motion, I gathered the strands of emotion and sensation and locked them deep inside, in a cage of thorned vines I wove within my mind. Aunt Caris would be well —and if she were not, I would help make her so. I drew in one deep breath, then another. I wouldn't surrender to these aberrations, not today, not as long as I kept the strength to resist. At last, my efforts brought silence, and the glasshouse became a refuge once more. I inhaled slowly, absorbing the familiar fragrances. Surely there was nothing objectionable in smelling the flowers.

The bitter acrimony of wormwood, ready to bite and purge, the soft perfume of lavender, ever-inclined to comfort and soothe, and the fresh, grassy scent of chamomile—all these and more wafted around me as I pulled a small pair of shears from their peg on the wall and made my way toward the table, which housed several varieties of lavender. I snipped a handful of buds, careful to remove only a little from each plant, in a manner that would encourage further growth.

And then a faint rustle broke through my enforced silence. I was so determined to shut out any possible aberration and give my attention only to gathering lavender, I almost ignored it. Until it came again, unmistakable, and followed by a slight moan.

I turned.

In the shadowed corner on the north wall, where the glasshouse nestled against our townhome, something stirred. My pulse picked up. I grabbed a shovel and crept forward.

Slowly, my sight adjusted to the relative dim. A large cat lurked beneath one of my plant shelves, in piteous condition. Bedraggled inky fur cloaked a body rent with wounds, and a tremendous thick tail matted with blood wrapped close round its bulky frame. What a dreadful scrap it must have endured.

A pale patch like a starflower spread across its chest, and from the torn face, jade eyes glared at me.

I cast the shovel aside and extended my hand.

It drew back with a hiss.

How on earth had the creature come to shelter here unseen? No matter; it needed aid. I spoke in a soothing undertone. "You're safe here. And if you let me closer, I can help."

I kept up a patter of reassurances as I fetched my leather gardening gloves—protection should the cat lash out. When I reached for it once more, it bared threatening fangs. I rocked back on my heels. "If you let me take you to the house, I'll see you well-tended. You must be hungry. I'm sure we have some fine scraps for you to enjoy . . . and maybe a bit of milk also?"

The stream of chatter appeared to calm it, so I continued. "It's clear you've fought well and come off with your life, and perhaps even the victory. But if I'm to help you now, you must allow me close."

The cat surveyed me, black pupils narrowing. And then, as if it understood, it dropped its stance of war and let its body slump.

I tucked the basket with the lavender buds in the crook of my elbow. Then I lifted the cat and cradled it to my chest. Even with both my arms wrapped securely around it, it spilled over, its head resting on my shoulder and its legs down low around my waist, its bulk unbalancing me at first. Not for the first time, I wished for a sturdier frame, but one must make the best of the resources given.

In this proximity to the cat, the earth-iron tang of old blood choked me, but I continued to murmur softly as I staggered into the house. In the washroom, I laid it down on a clean towel.

"Stay here—I'll be back."

I hurried down the stairs to the lowest level, which housed the kitchen. The honeyed fragrance of baking pastries wafted out to greet me. Our cook, Estine—thin as a reed despite her frequent sampling of her own wares—had a deft touch with all manner of baked goods and prided herself on turning them out fresh to accompany every meal. She'd served our family since Mother and Father wed, and after Mother's death she'd sought to comfort all three of us girls by inviting us into the warm bustle of her kitchen.

When I crossed the threshold, she turned with a welcoming smile that faded the moment she saw me. "Mercies, Miss Jessa. Are you hurt?"

I glanced down at my front. Blood streaked the pale muslin of my gown, likely creating indelible stains. Small wonder I had startled her. "It's not my blood. I found an injured cat in the glasshouse."

"And you just had to wrangle it, did you?" She examined me more closely, a frown creasing her face. "You're certain it didn't scratch you? It might well carry all sorts of disease."

"It's not ill, only injured. And I couldn't leave it there to die."

She brushed flour from her hands. "Mebbe not, but Ives could have fetched the creature for you, I'm sure. No need for you to muss yourself, Miss Jessa, none at all."

"It was simple enough for me to handle the situation without the aid of a footman." I placed the basket of lavender on the long table in the center of the room. "I've only come for hot water and some rags. Once I've tended the cat, I'll return to make some tea for Aunt Caris, if you don't mind setting out the tray."

Muttering under her breath about the fate of those ladies inclined toward independence and wild risks—as if the simple matter of attending an injured animal was the equivalent of venturing into the heart of a Crossing—she filled a pitcher and passed it to me, along with a basin and a few worn linens.

Then I went to the stillroom where I stored my dried herbs and fetched some valerian root. Armed for possible battle, I returned to the washroom.

The cat still rested on the towel, but it inclined its head toward me when I entered, a surprisingly regal gesture given its condition. I offered the valerian, my best hope of calming it enough to tend its wounds. It pricked its ears toward the pungent-smelling root and nibbled the herb, its body gradually easing into a state of relaxation. The shift in position revealed that despite her size, the cat was female. If she was willing to stay, she'd need a name, but that could come later.

Though she wouldn't be able to understand, I quietly presented the facts, assuring her I intended only to help, though the process might be painful. She batted my arm with her paw, and then returned to her rest. After I drew in a breath to steady myself, I cleansed the cuts on her face, working slowly toward the worst of the wounds—a long rent down her side, clotted in places, seeping in others.

Though the cat gave a low moan as I tended her injuries, she didn't strike out. For whatever reason, she'd decided to trust me, or at least not fight my attempts to render aid. At last, with the deepest gash bandaged and slathered with a thick unguent and the lesser cuts and scrapes anointed with a lighter salve, I bundled the cat, towel and all, into my arms and climbed the numerous stairs to my bedchamber, located on the third floor of our town house. Slightly out of breath, I placed the cat on a cushioned chair.

Now for Aunt Caris.

After I scrubbed up and changed my gown, I went back to the kitchen, where the basket of lavender awaited. As I steeped the buds and willow bark together, my mind drifted to Aunt Caris's peculiar reaction. How could I convince her to share whatever concerned her and allow me to help shoulder the load? Given her voluble nature, I'd never had to pry information from her before. I'd simply have to venture forward one step at a time.

I only hoped my delay hadn't added to her worries. I swiftly placed the pot of tea on the tray Estine had prepared and climbed the stairs once more.

I eased open the door to Aunt Caris's bedchamber. If by chance she was sleeping, I'd leave the herbal infusion at her bedside table and return later. I had no reason to fear rousing her since she slept so deeply even a dragon incursion wouldn't cause her to stir, let alone my presence in her bedchamber.

But she was not even abed, much less asleep. The heavy drapes, in the greens and florals she favored, were pulled back to allow the sun to pour in, and she stood by the exposed window, motionless, staring into the bustling street below. The first calling hours had reached their zenith, and carriages rattled over cobblestones in ceaseless procession before the long rows of townhomes.

I walked to her side. "Aunt Caris, I've brought the infusion for your headache."

"Thank you, dear." She half-turned toward me.

Were those tearstains on her cheeks? I tightened my grip on the tea tray.

"If it's not too much trouble, will you ask Ives to bring my trunk from the attic?" she asked. "I'll be leaving in the morning for Milburn, and I want to prepare as soon as possible."

I set down the tray with a clink on the bedside table. "Milburn? I don't believe I've heard the name before. Is it far from here?"

"I've never been there, but I suppose it will be a bit of an expedition . . ." Aunt Caris paused a moment, and in the distance a multitude of oratory bells sounded the hour. "It's near the Morven Crossing."

Given the location, her reluctance to confess was unsurprising. No true Crossing towns remained in the kingdom of Byren. After several had vanished or been destroyed by Otherkind centuries ago, the rest had been abandoned, by edict of the king. Edgetowns skirted the nebulous border around each Crossing, a fifteen-mile radius recommended by the Vigilists for reasons unexplained to us ordinary mortals. Though edgetowns offered the reward of rich resources, the potential for Otherkind incursions meant they also held great risk. Such invasions had become rare—the Vigilists posited that we experienced relative peace due to some unknown Otherworld cycle—but still, one must embrace the prospect of danger to settle there, and indeed, their citizens not infrequently vanished or suffered inexplicable calamity. Mother'd had no qualms about the risks surrounding Crossings, else she would not have purchased Thornhaven shortly after she'd wed Father, but he decidedly disagreed.

I poured the tea and handed her a steaming cup. "Why Milburn . . . and with such urgency?"

"A friend has found herself in a great difficulty and written to request my assistance." She accepted the mug, and it quavered in her unsteady grasp, nearly spilling tea over the edge.

Her distress indicated something troubled her beyond just a friend in need. What did she conceal?

"So you plan to travel to an edgetown alone?" Viewed by society as a spinster, she required no chaperone. But to undertake a journey beyond the comforts of the more settled regions, particularly without accompaniment, was unlike her. Not to mention that she would endure a longer, more arduous trip by carriage since steam trains kept a great distance from any Crossing to protect their investments from possible damage.

"I'll take Ives. Between him and the coachman, I'll be safe enough." The fine lines around her eyes deepened, hinting at inward strain. "And since Melisina is relying on you and your sisters for aid in planning her annual spring fete, I thought it best to make the journey on my own rather than disrupt her plans."

Of course Aunt Caris would put her own comfort aside rather than face Aunt Melisina's wrath. Few dared disturb the arrangements Aunt Melisina made. I studied her. "Ada and Ainslie may be essential to her fete, but I'd only planned to aid with the flower arrangements, which she can easily hire out. She won't miss me, at least not sufficiently to protest."

Once more I blessed the fact that the entrance of my sisters into society—and their determination *not* to accept the proposals that had come their way thus far—allowed the delay of my own formal appearance. I couldn't push it off forever, but for now, my presence was not required.

"But I couldn't possibly ask you to—"

"You're not asking, I'm offering." If Aunt Caris thought I intended to make any sort of sacrifice on her behalf, she'd turn me down flat. So I forced eagerness into my tone, despite my concerns about the trip. "I've always wanted to travel in the Dythe Mountain territory, and if Milburn is near the Morven Crossing, it must at least have mountain views. I imagine they'll also have some uncommon flowers and shrubs. It would be delightful to add some new sketches to my collection, and perhaps I could even bring a few plants home for our gardens."

Never mind that the garden of our townhome in Avons brimmed with life, every corner and crevice overflowing with flowers, herbs, and trees in exuberant array. If I was creative enough, I might fit in a few more.

A shadow passed over her face. "The trip may be tiring."

"All the more reason for me to accompany you. The journey will be much less arduous with a companion." I offered a bright smile.

"I'm afraid . . . the letter . . ." She stared into her teacup as if it held solutions to whatever plagued her. "My friend seems deeply disturbed. She may not be as amiable as usual. How can I bring you into what could be a difficult situation?"

"Quite easily."

She shook her head.

"Aunt Caris, please let me come."

"What will your father say?"

"He can spare me for a fortnight, surely."

"It may be longer than that. But perhaps . . . if he agrees . . ." She sipped at the infusion, and a bit of the tension eased from her shoulders.

"I'm certain he will." Father might miss my assistance in keeping up with his correspondence and organizing his work, but otherwise, he'd be unlikely to rouse himself from his studies long enough to object. I breathed in the aroma of lavender drifting up from the teapot, but it failed to bring a sense of calm. "I'll ask Ives to fetch our trunks and then speak with Father."

She gripped my hand with her free one. "Thank you, dear."

I pressed a kiss to her temple and fled the room, chased by the question: what awaited us in Milburn?

CHAPTER 2

With permission from Father secured and supplies packed, all that remained was to take our leave. Shortly after dawn, I coaxed the cat into a large cushioned basket I'd prepared for her travels and draped it with a blanket. Ives had already fetched my luggage and loaded it into the carriage, so I donned my hat and gloves and left my bedchamber to join Aunt Caris.

I'd just reached the first landing when a cry interrupted my progress.

"Wait!"

Ainslie hastened to join me, Ada following at a more sedate pace behind. Despite the early hour, they were as immaculately arrayed as morning glories, every dark curl woven into place with creamy ribbons and every line of their ivory gowns falling in graceful contours to the floor. In short, they were striking. Small wonder Aunt Melisina enjoyed ushering them through society given that both their words and deeds matched their appearance.

Ainslie flitted to my side, her gauzy skirt swirling about her ankles. "Did you think we'd let you leave without saying goodbye?"

"You were out so late with Aunt Melisina, I thought you'd rather sleep."

"Nonsense. These hours may be more suited to birds than to mortals, but we'd not forgo seeing you off for anything." Ainslie wrapped me in a fierce embrace, her wild-rose fragrance swirling about me.

Ada followed up with a gentler hug. "Do be sure to stop before dark every night, and when you reach Milburn, take care to always wear your ward-pendant."

"Of course." No matter that she was only two years my elder, Ada could never resist mothering. She even succumbed to the temptation with her twin Ainslie. "Aunt Caris and I have planned every stop along the way."

"Wonderful." Then shadows darkened her deep-brown eyes. "But have Simms and Ives their pistols?"

"They do, indeed." I adjusted the heavy basket. "I'm certain we'll be fine."

Ainslie wrapped an arm around Ada. "Never fear, sister. You know Aunt Caris. She wouldn't take the trip if she believed there were any danger."

Under usual circumstances, I'd agree with Ainslie, but something in the letter had impacted Aunt Caris enough for her to forsake her usual caution and determine to travel to Milburn at once. Recalling her letter brought to mind my own, one that must go to Ibbie in my absence. I set down the basket and rummaged in my reticule. "I have a letter for Lady Dromley. Would you see it goes out in the morning post? She's expecting me this afternoon to sketch an artifact recovered from a site near Bervale."

"Of course." Ada accepted it, and a faint furrow creased her brow. "She certainly keeps you occupied."

"I don't mind." Because, unlike my family, Ibbie appreciated my desire to learn, to understand, to bury myself in study. The same spark kindled in her, only her interests lay in the realm of antiquarian matters. "They're rather fascinating."

"I daresay they have something to recommend them, but I cannot imagine you'd forsake your plants for her antiquities," Ainslie said.

I laughed. "Fortunately, that's not required."

Such a deed would be impossible, for I'd certainly tried. Though cutting myself off from botanical life had diminished the whispers, it had also deadened something inside me. The world had lost its savor, becoming bleak and gray. Even my appetite had vanished. So I embraced the risks for the reward offered.

"And if you did, who would see our house so strikingly adorned with blooms?" Ada inclined her head. "Lady Tilsbury was much struck by your arrangements and declared our garden the envy of Avons. She was quite impressed when we told her it was all due to your efforts."

Impressed? Or merely polite enough to hide her disdain at such a commonplace pursuit? Either way, Ada had credited me as a kindness, so I reached out and squeezed her hand. "I'm glad you enjoy them." Then I lifted my basket once more. "I don't wish to keep Aunt Caris waiting."

The three of us descended the final flight together and joined Aunt Caris in the entry.

"We will miss you both," Ada said.

Aunt Caris patted Ada's arm. "We won't be long, my dear. I've no desire to linger in the wilds of Milburn."

Then Ainslie prodded the enormous basket in my arms.

"What *are* you toting in here, Jessa? A year's worth of sketchbooks? Or an entire collection of treatises on edgetowns?"

"Not quite." A smile tugged at the corners of my mouth, and I pulled back the blanket to reveal the inhabitant of the basket. "Only the cat I found in the glasshouse yesterday. She's injured and needs tending."

"You truly mean to bring that creature with us?" Aunt Caris asked.

I nodded. "She won't let any of the maids near her, and I don't wish to add to the burden of the household in our absence."

Aunt Caris peered into the basket. "She's a bit disreputable in appearance."

The cat's brilliant eyes narrowed, and her ears twitched back, almost as though she understood the criticism—and resented it.

"She's been badly injured, but once she's healed, she'll be magnificent." Though even fully recovered, she'd never appear like a proper pet. The ladies who preferred cats to dogs favored the long-haired, pure white or golden breeds for pets, those with petite features and dainty airs—not enormous black beasts.

The cat nudged my hand and gave a soft *mrow*.

Ainslie laughed. "It appears she agrees. She certainly seems to favor you."

"Who wouldn't appreciate their rescuer?" Ada offered a sparkling smile, then lifted a smaller basket draped over her own arm. "When Aunt Caris told us you'd be departing this morning, I asked Estine to assemble a basket with some of your favorites so you'd be well-supplied for the road."

"How thoughtful, my dear." Aunt Caris accepted it and then kissed Ada and Ainslie on the cheek. "Now we really must be going if we wish to reach the inn by evening. I'm of no mind to spend the night within the carriage."

"Never fear, I'm certain Simms will see you there with all haste. I've never known him to decline a warm bed and a pint." Ainslie leaned forward, and her scar glinted in the morning light that poured through the arched transom above the door, a reminder that I'd yet to render her the promised aid. "Please say you'll write, even if you return home before your letters, as we hope."

"Of course." Aunt Caris donned her hat and secured the ribbons beneath her chin.

After one more round of embraces, we were on our way, rattling down the lane in a hired carriage, with Simms at the helm and Ives alongside him.

I turned and caught one final glimpse of Ada and Ainslie standing on the doorstep, arms linked, waving farewell. Then we rounded a bend, and they vanished from sight.

As the horses trotted down Camden Row, its scents swirled into the carriage: the pale, dry aroma of sun-warmed sovstone mingling with the sharp scent of the gas lamps and the sweet-orange smell of the alchemical solution used to keep the door-stones gleaming white.

The fragrances were pleasant enough, at least in this sector of Avons, but elsewhere . . . I'd traversed some areas of the city that made me long for a return to Caldwell House and Upper North-lea. What would await in Milburn? Would I find the sights and smells familiar or foreign?

I returned my attention to Aunt Caris, intending to inquire about her friend and what might await. But she must have spent a sleepless night, for she'd already drifted into a deep slumber, whiffling out a snore now and then that rustled the ribbons of her hat.

As we wove past residential streets and into the market district of Avons, I ran a finger down the center of the cat's head, one of the few unscathed regions on her body. "What shall I call you?"

She surveyed me with luminous green eyes, her pupils slitted in the bright morning light.

"Jade, perhaps, after your eyes?"

A rumbling purr resounded in her chest, and I took it as a sign of approval.

"Jade it is, then." I stroked her once more, considering her unusual appearance and conduct. She didn't act like a feral cat, nor was she skin and bones as they often were, but neither did she carry herself with the gentle amiability of a pet. Where had she come from before she received her injuries? What had brought her to shelter in the glasshouse? I leaned back. "I suppose I'll never know."

She regarded me a long moment, her head tilted to one side. Then she hopped up to the window, surveying the passing scenery.

Once outside the confines of Avons, our surroundings thrummed with new life. On the edge of the road, brilliant yellow cowslips bobbed in the breeze, singing in bright, chirpy notes. Beneath a stand of oaks, violets crept, breathing a promise to ease the heart and gladden the soul . . .

No, no, no.

I must be more nervous about this expedition than I wished to acknowledge. I clenched my hands around my reticule, the embroidered knots digging into my skin, and willed them all to silence. I would not listen, nor would I hear. Not unless I wanted to face the Vigil.

Compared to their involvement, attention from gossips and scandalmongers would be only a minor affliction. I couldn't imagine the Vigilists would be amenable to the argument Father offered regarding my condition. They were swift to leap to accusations of fae-touch and force the individuals so afflicted into their Institutions, claiming the act vital for the protection of the kingdom. After all, if madness were the inevitable result of fae-touch, quick action was required.

Two decades didn't offer one much experience in the world, but it had provided me time enough to witness their deeds . . . and however well they guarded Byren, the Vigilists had also left suffering in their wake. But to remember would not bring calm. I forced myself to relax my grip on the reticule.

Then I warded myself against the onslaught with care, locking my emotions deep within. All my life, this practice of imagining a cage of thorns, woven tight enough to contain all unruly sensation, had been effective, but now the figurative vines felt fragile, likely to crumble against the force battering them. If the force were malicious rather than alluring, it might be easier to resist. Instead, it beckoned, so sweetly . . . no, I refused to allow such thoughts room. I envisioned another cord of thorns binding around the others and exhaled in the blessed silence.

Mrow. Jade batted at my arm.

"Are you hungry?" I rummaged in a small basket at my feet and withdrew a bit of dried fish I'd packed for her.

She crunched down on it with satisfaction, and I kept my gaze on her rather than allowing it to drift to the scenery beyond the window. When she joined Aunt Caris in slumber, I immersed myself in a book of conundrums, finding satisfaction in every successful solution. With each answer uncovered, the tension eased a bit from my shoulders. Fortunately, conundrums weren't considered an unladylike pastime, unlike my efforts to assist Ibbie in solving her antiquarian mysteries. Her lofty status in society allowed her more liberties than most, and she'd used it to sway my aunts into acceptance of my involvement in her antiquarian affairs. Moreover, she'd proven herself a champion for my works as well as her own, ever-confident my manuscript would meet with success, no matter the repeated rejections it had received. Though she relied upon me to sketch her artifacts, she'd have been the first to support my desire to accompany Aunt Caris, as Ibbie's own lack of family pained her deeply.

I folded back the page to uncover a new conundrum and attended to the puzzles within until Aunt Caris roused herself at midday. Though she appeared well-rested and in better spirits, she still deflected all my attempts to find out what awaited us in Milburn. What her friend expected Aunt Caris to do—and the nature of the problem itself—remained a mystery.

Over the days we traveled, I read the numerous tomes I'd brought, sketched the passing scenery, and listened to Aunt Caris effusively converse on every topic except the troubles we would face. When we finally neared Milburn, I renewed my efforts.

"Aunt Caris, if we're to help your friend, perhaps you could tell me what's troubling her?"

"There's no need for you to be drawn into her difficulties, dear." She patted my hand absently, her attention locked on a world within. "You've been wonderful company, and that's all I ask. I'm sure there'll be plenty of scenic views around the village for you to sketch while I call on Melle."

Melle. I finally had a name . . . and no intention of avoiding the situation. For something was sorely amiss, as evidenced by the abstraction Aunt Caris displayed as we drew closer to Milburn. If she were feeling herself, she'd be commenting on the beauty of the land around us and her anticipation over the end of our journey. After a long stretch over a narrow, densely forested road, the way broadened and fields opened around us.

Through the carriage window, I surveyed the rolling hills, some cleared and dotted with sheep, others covered with ancient stands of trees. Something about our surroundings reminded me of Thornhaven. Never mind that I hadn't stayed there since I was eight years old—the memories remained vivid. Mother had chosen to purchase the long-abandoned property with her own resources, despite its poor situation near Aelfgard Crossing, and she'd lovingly restored it. She'd visited twice a year without fail and brought us children along as a matter of course. She'd even persuaded Father to come as well. Despite his reluctance to stay in the shadow of a Crossing, his love for her had moved him toward her desires. In her will, she'd left Thornhaven in trust for Ada, Ainslie, and me. Perhaps she'd known Father might have sold it off otherwise. However, though it belonged to us, Father forbade us to return in his fear that some untimely fate might befall us.

If his distraction over the article he was writing for the Royal Mathematical Society hadn't kept him from inquiring about where we intended to travel, doubtless he would have forbidden this journey as well. He might even have tried to sway Aunt Caris, though she would have taken no heed.

As we crested a hill, I caught my first glimpse of Milburn, its tall buildings of local graystone constructed with dark, steeply arched rooflines and colorful doors. The town fit seamlessly into the vale, mirroring the mountains beyond, and I ached to capture the picturesque scene on paper. I could have soaked in the beauty of the unfolding view for hours, but we passed through at a steady clip, Aunt Caris eager to reach our destination.

Our coachman halted the team outside an inn bearing a sign: *The White Hart*. I leaned forward to get a clearer view. In appearance, the inn resembled the homes we'd passed, though much larger, its three stories all solid graystone with elegant ironwork, kept from a forbidding appearance by generous window boxes brimming with colorful blossoms and double doors of a rich green hue standing open to welcome all comers.

The courtyard itself resembled a hive of bees bothered by an inexpert keeper, all in a welter of disturbed activity. What so bestirred the inn? Or was this their customary way? No one noticed our waiting carriage till our coachman forcibly secured an ostler to tend the horses. As was proper, Ives opened the door and stood beside the stairs to offer assistance. After I disembarked, I turned to fetch Jade's basket. I lifted it, the handle digging into my arms. Even contained, Jade proved an unwieldy burden, yet she was already becoming dear to me, and her presence had provided a pleasant distraction throughout our journey.

Aunt Caris brushed a few wrinkles from her forest-green traveling skirt and then my own, never mind that our gowns needed a thorough wash and pressing to be truly presentable. Then she pinned up a wayward dark curl—one of the few features I shared with my sisters—before patting my cheek and releasing me.

When we approached the open door of the inn, we passed a tall man with black hair and a graying beard who attempted to bring order to the chaos. His left shoulder bore a stratesman's insignia, by which authority, apparently, he held at bay the knot of angry individuals before him.

"She must be held to account." A bull of a man folded thick arms. "Lest she endanger us all."

A small, pale woman stood alongside the stratesman, shrinking back from the accusatory voices, timorous as a mouse caught in a snare.

Blight and rot, what was happening here?

"My dear, we'd best go into the inn." Aunt Caris tugged my arm. "This sort of altercation is no place for a lady."

I allowed her to sweep me through the doorway, which bore a prominent ward-stone to guard against hostile fae intrusion, and into the well-appointed welcoming room. Overstuffed chairs clustered around a large hearth, inviting guests to take their ease. Across from the hearth stood a polished oak counter with a row of keys hanging beyond, left unattended for the moment. A large fountain, stylized to look like a forest pool, with harts graven along its sides, provided a peaceful burbling sound in the background. This close to Morven Crossing, I imagined the innkeepers sought to garner as much favor as possible with any nisi who might choose to dwell concealed here.

From the depths of the inn, a sonsy, dark-haired woman bustled over to greet us. She resembled a peony, her flushed pink-and-white features blooming with fulsome charm.

"Welcome. I'm Mrs. Wilkins. I'm afraid we're at odds and ends at the moment, but we'll get you set to rights in no time." She extended her hands, palms up in greeting. "You'll be wanting a suite with a private dining room, I expect?"

Aunt Caris nodded. "And we require accommodations for our footman and coachman as well."

"Certainly, we'll see to it." She fetched several keys. "Now, if you'll just come with me."

She led us up a flight of stairs, down whitewashed corridors with woven indigo-and-gray rugs, and then up once more. Off the second landing clustered a suite of rooms, more welcoming and homelike than I expected. The furnishings were simple and practical, pleasing to the eye with their sturdy, well-cut lines and dark tones, but lacking the ornamentation one would find in Avons.

I set the basket containing Jade on an oval table and rolled my shoulders to ease the strain of her weight. She slitted one eye to peer about the room, then stretched with an improved range of motion. The days of travel, during which she'd remained mostly immobile, had worked wonders on her injuries.

Mrs. Wilkins beamed at us with the confidence of one who knew she maintained a pleasing standard of hospitality. "Will these rooms suit?"

Aunt Caris stood motionless at her post near the window, looking out toward the river as if mesmerized by its distant shimmer.

My shoulders tightened. If she couldn't observe the usual pleasantries, then her worries must have returned to plague her tenfold. I turned to Mrs. Wilkins. "Yes, they're quite lovely."

Most likely, these were their nicest accommodations, given that each bedchamber was accompanied by a narrow sitting room and joined by a private dining chamber between. Yet my eye caught on the one peculiarity in the rooms—interior shutters fashioned of scrolled iron. While intricate in pattern, their worn hinges and the slightly chipped paint around the window frames suggested they were designed for use.

I ran my finger over one of the scrolls, and its unnatural cold made me shiver.

Perhaps taking note of my interest, Mrs. Wilkins hastened to the windows and demonstrated how to secure the shutters. "We send our maidservants through to latch the shutters at dusk every evening, but in case you should want to do them yourselves earlier, it's simple enough. No sense extending an open invitation for fae to come prowling."

Aunt Caris clutched her reticule closer. "No, indeed."

"We also suggest that our guests confine their exploration of Milburn to the daylight hours and stay to the town proper. We don't want to lose anyone unnecessarily." She pulled the shutters open once more and offered another of her friendly smiles, as though she'd not just made my blood run cold. "What time does it please you to dine tonight?"

"We keep early hours," I said. "Six will suit."

"Very well. If you need anything, only ring, and Eda will see you're attended." She adjusted a tilting pinkslip in the vase on the table and then prepared to leave.

"One moment." Aunt Caris crossed the room to join us. "Could you give us directions to Dyott Mill? How far is it from the inn?"

Mrs. Wilkins started, then folded her arms across her ample bosom. "Dyott Mill? Why do you ask?"

"A friend of mine owns the mill."

"You're speaking of Melle Hopkins?" Mrs. Wilkins shifted her weight from one foot to the other. "She may be a friend, but you'll find yourself sharing her woes if you don't have a care. Best stay away."

If an innkeeper's wife had dared address her so, Aunt Melisina would have delivered one of her famous setdowns, but Aunt Caris only drew closer, her brow creased. "Why do you say that?"

Mrs. Wilkins's lips compressed into a firm line. "There's peculiar goings-on at the mill, and the stratesman won't do what he must and arrest her who's responsible."

"Then he knows the culprit?"

"Who else could it be but her who lived there before?" Mrs. Wilkins sighed. "The double tragedy addled her wits, and no surprise."

My mind leapt back to the frightened woman in front of the inn. "Are you referring to the girl who was outside with the stratesman when we arrived?"

"That's the one, and it's sorry I am you had to witness that."

Her flush deepened. "She had the audacity to try to stay here. *Here*, of all places. I run a proper inn, not a madhouse."

The woman hadn't looked mad, only frightened and forlorn. I checked the protest that rose to my lips. I knew nothing of the situation, not yet, but I did know better than most how deeply one could conceal the truth when necessary.

Aunt Caris stole a glance at me. "Yes, well, I must see my friend, but we'll exercise the proper care."

"As it pleases you, Miss Caldwell." But Mrs. Wilkins gave a disapproving shake of her head. "I've no wish to see any of my guests come to harm, but your business is your own, I'm certain. I'll send Eda with water for washing up."

When she departed, I faced Aunt Caris—it was past time for some answers. "Harm? What's happened to your friend? I thought you said she experienced difficulties, not danger."

"Well, I . . ." She plucked at the lace on the neckline of her gown. "I didn't think there was danger precisely, just some sort of . . . sabotage. Melle didn't offer much detail in her letter, only that she required assistance."

"I see." But I did not. Aunt Caris had always been open and easy to read, but the discomfort in every line of her body suggested concealment. What did she wish to keep hidden? And why? Did she fear betraying a confidence entrusted her by her friend? Surely she knew I'd not speak out of turn.

She waved her hand. "Enough of that for now. You know how these small towns are—I'm sure they've gossiped endlessly, making a great deal more of the matter than it warrants. I'll call on Melle tomorrow and get the facts, while you go out sketching."

"Aunt Caris." I took both her hands in mine. "You can't truly expect I'll gad about Milburn while you face a possible threat?"

"I'm sure it will be fine, dear." Though she maintained a light tone, she refused to meet my eyes.

"Then there's no harm in my coming." I rarely insisted on my way against the wishes of my family, but I refused to let her go on her own. I might not bring the vivacity Ada and Ainslie would if they were here, their light banter making Aunt Caris smile and forget her woes, but I could offer companionship and support. "And if it turns out I'm not needed, the mill will be as charming a sketching location as the town."

Her brow furrowed. "Melle may not be pleased to have additional company. Best let me go alone, my dear."

I forced myself to press through the discomfort of edging in where I wasn't wanted. "It's clear the townsfolk feel something troublesome is stirring, and you shouldn't face it alone. Would you let me venture into an unchancy situation on my own?"

She blinked rapidly. "That's different."

"Do you doubt I care as much for your safety as you do mine?"

"Of course not, dear." She fidgeted with her lace again, clearly seeking some excuse to keep me within Milburn proper. "I suppose if you wish—"

"It's settled, then." I walked over to my trunk and prepared to unpack. The scent of the rose and lavender sachets tucked within the clothes soothed slightly the sting of her intended rejection. Whatever problems lay ahead at Dyott Mill, we'd face them together—whether Aunt Caris wished it or not.

CHAPTER 3

When we departed for Dyott Mill the next morning, the courtyard was tranquil, as if the disturbance of the day before had been just a dream. Few people stirred at this early hour, and only the soft whicker of horses in the stable and the murmurs of the stable hands broke the silence. Dew shimmered on the stone pavers and the trees beyond, as if the world had received a baptism of peace overnight.

Oh, how I wished I could absorb that peace into myself. My stomach churned whenever I thought of the conflict that lay ahead. Though Aunt Caris had divulged the bare facts of the situation, she kept much concealed—enough to leave me feeling entirely unprepared for the day before us. I liked answers and information, connecting puzzle pieces to see the full picture, not charging in blindly with a tiny fragment of fact that might fit any variety of situations.

Our carriage passed through tidy rows of buildings on cobbled lanes. Homes and shops alike were well-ordered and maintained, a veneer of civilization applied to cover the true nature of the land beneath, which throbbed with a hint of *Other,* a thorn-pricking sensation akin to what I experienced at times in the garden or glasshouse, a relentless urge to surrender to the unknown.

"What do you think of Milburn?" Aunt Caris asked as we rattled over the streets. She donned an air of good cheer like one might a domino for a masquerade. It was all the more discomfiting, because in ordinary times, she wore it without effort, the natural outflow of a pleasant, contented soul.

In truth, my fingers itched to sketch everything I saw—the graystone houses and shops, the bountiful gardens, the bustling market we passed, and most of all, the tremendous trees bordering the town and the rolling hills sweeping beyond. "It's charming. I'm glad I came."

She adjusted her hat to conceal her eyes. "I'm thankful as well, my dear."

Even as she spoke, the thorn-pricking sensation intensified. Dared I inquire about it? Would doing so reveal more than I wished? If only I knew what was common and what was . . . peculiar. I attended to keeping my voice light, as though the answer to my question mattered not at all. "Aunt Caris, do you think edgetowns hold some element of the Otherworld— perhaps some power of their own?"

"Gracious, my dear, the questions you ask." She brushed at her forest-green gown as if to remove invisible dust. "I can't imagine so, else surely the Vigil would have banned them from habitation. They would never have risked Otherworldly influence over our people."

"So it doesn't feel any . . . different to you here?"

"No, indeed not." Concern shaded her eyes. "Why do you ask?"

Because the taint within me might have gained strength with

proximity to the Crossing, might be seeking to blossom in new ways. I choked back my fears. "I was just curious."

It was a testament to her preoccupation about the plight of her friend that she fell into silence, rather than pressing for answers, and in the quiet, I examined the world unfolding outside our windows. As long as my cage of thorns held secure, I could enjoy the scenery. I made some quick sketches of soft fern fronds, their unfurling tips tinted red, and of white wood anemone blossoming beneath a cluster of elms. The familiar motions lulled me into a pleasant dreamy state, removed from whatever trouble might lay ahead—until a cry of terror pierced the stillness.

I jumped, ripping my pencil across the page. A long, jagged rent formed in the wake of the lead, and I stared insensibly at it, my pulse surging. Aunt Caris jolted upright, and the carriage picked up its pace.

Frantic shouts tore the air, followed by the sound of a woman keening. Blight and rot, what lay in wait?

The carriage lurched to a halt, and Ives appeared at the window. "We've neared the mill, but we daren't go any closer, Miss Caldwell."

"Gracious, what now?" Aunt Caris clenched her hands in her lap, knuckles whitening. "I suppose we must disembark here. Is it safe?"

"If you have a care."

He opened the door, and we emerged into a realm of confusion. Before the mill cottage, a tremendous sinkhole gaped, filled with dark, rippling water. Two women grappled before it, one attempting to hold the other back, and a pair of young boys clung to each other nearer the house.

Aunt Caris turned to Ives. "We must help. Go quickly."

Help with what? By the Crossings, what had happened here?

To his credit, Ives charged forward. We rushed in his wake, but as we approached, the earth grew water-softened and unstable.

The taller of the two women nearly lost her grasp on the other, and she shouted, "Stop fighting me! If you go, we lose you too. Think of Jan and Daw."

"Think of Essie!" The smaller woman wailed the words.

At that moment a soft laugh, laced with malice, whispered on the wind. I staggered backward and whipped my head around, seeking the source of the sound.

But there was no one.

No time to consider the implications, not now.

For at the sinkhole's edge, I glimpsed a small hand. Then it vanished into the dark waters. Everything clicked into place. A child, drowning. A mother, willing to save her, prevented by another. *We lose you too.* She must be unable to swim, but of course she would risk everything. For a mother without a child —oh, it was as unbearable as a child without a mother.

My chest constricted.

Faint laughter still echoing in my ears, I sprinted forward, stumbling in the soft earth, righting myself. I reached the edge. And without another thought, I plunged into the sinkhole. I expected—hoped—my feet would touch bottom, but nothing.

How deep did the fault run?

I dove into the darkly clouded waters. As I traveled down, fumbling along the rock-and-soil edge, the peculiar vase shape of the sinkhole revealed itself, narrow at the opening, wide beneath. Treacherous.

The girl could be trapped beneath the ledge, unable to rise. If I didn't find her . . .

My pulse pounded in my ears. I shot to the surface, gasped a breath. Then dove deeper.

A ripple tugged at me, some sort of disturbance in the

waters. I followed, propelling myself beneath the ledge of earth. Below this ridge, I searched blindly. I must find her. I must.

My body demanded air, but I thrust the need aside. Just a little longer.

My fingers brushed something soft, nubbly. Wool? I drove myself forward, reaching, reaching . . .

There.

I snagged a tiny arm and tugged, but the child didn't budge. Was it already too late? I pulled harder.

Nothing.

She must be caught on something in the waters below. I gripped her torso and yanked, my lungs screaming for air. Still no movement. I traced her body, seeking the source of entrapment.

If only whatever it was would *release*.

Sudden and swift as the snapping of a thread, she broke free. Her body collided with mine, tiny and limp. Lungs burning, I surged back to the surface with the girl clasped close. I hauled in one breath, then another.

She did not.

Ives waited at the edge with the older woman. I gripped the rope they extended, and he dragged us from the waters.

The young girl's form remained limp, unmoving. In the light of day, she looked so small, scarcely more than a babe—and so fragile.

Oh please, please breathe.

The older woman tilted the girl so her feet rose above her head, then compressed her abdomen once, twice, three times. At last, she coughed, sputtered, and began to wail.

I sank to my knees. *Infinite be praised.* Never had a cry sounded so sweet.

We slipped through the muck at the edge of the sinkhole

onto firmer terrain, and the younger woman surged forward. She grabbed the girl and examined every inch of her, covering her with kisses, and murmuring incoherent reassurance.

Ives returned to Aunt Caris and lent her a hand over the treacherous ground. With care, they skirted the sinkhole and joined us before the cottage. Though he assisted her, his gaze kept straying back to me. I folded my arms across my front, uncomfortable with the way my wet gown clung to me before an audience.

"Oh, my dear." Aunt Caris hovered over me like a hen might an injured chick. "Are you well?"

"I'm fine, Aunt Caris." Or I would be, in time . . . when the sensation of that tiny body pressed against mine faded. I stifled a shiver.

"Thank the Infinite." She touched my cheek as if to assure herself. "If you were harmed, I would have never forgiven myself for having brought you here."

Then she turned to the older woman. "What happened, Melle?"

"We'd been letting out the sheep." The older woman—Melle —spoke slowly, her dark head bowed. "The children ran ahead, back to the house. And then this—"

She glowered at the abyss. "It just . . . opened before them. Nary a sign we'd had before that it might come. The boys were nearer the cottage, but Essie, she was too close to the edge. She fell."

The early spring air pebbled my skin, and this time, I couldn't restrain a shiver.

The younger woman looked up, her misty gray eyes awash with tears. "None of us can swim. I thought to go after her anyway, but Mother was right. I'd never have succeeded. If you hadn't arrived when you did . . ." She buried her face in her daughter's hair.

I rubbed my arms in a vain attempt to warm myself. "I'm thankful I could help."

Melle tucked away any sign of emotion, straightening her body into a stance of rigid control. "Come into the house with you. You can get out of those wet clothes while Caris and I have words."

Her statement sounded ominous, almost like a threat. Nevertheless, I stumbled behind her into the blessedly warm cottage.

A tiny woman with wispy white hair and skin as withered as an old apple waited in the doorway. Her attention was fixed on the sinkhole, and her expression of keen interest left me discomfited.

Melle linked her arm through the woman's and led her inside. "Auntie, you should return to your room and lie down. The excitement's no good for you."

"I've told you, Mellie. They wait. They wait to—"

"That's quite enough." Melle turned to the oldest boy. "Jan, take Auntie to rest."

He tugged her hand, steering her into the depths of the cottage, and Melle led us into the kitchen, where a fire blazed in the hearth. An iron kettle hung on a hook, already steaming, and Melle prepared tea while the young mother tended Essie, billing and cooing over her like a dove with a beloved squab.

In contrast, Melle clattered the tea things with a force that caused Aunt Caris to lift a brow. She firmly believed a lady never raised a ruckus and undoubtedly worked hard to restrain any sign of disapproval. Though the two of them must be of a similar age, there the similarities ended. Melle was all stark lines and angles, strength showing in the muscles that corded her hands and arms, her tightly-bound ebony hair only just streaking with a few strands of white, while Aunt Caris was fashioned of soft, gentle curves, with dimpled arms and cheeks and coppery hair swept into the latest style, her elegant curls clustered around her face. How had they come to share acquaintance?

While the tea steeped, Melle fetched me a blanket and some clean garments. "These will be a bit too large for you, but they'll keep you from getting a chill."

"Thank you." I stepped into the storeroom adjacent to the kitchen to change my clothes. They were simpler than my own, but dry and warm, which was all I required.

Melle's voice drifted through the wall. "It's time we talked, Caris. Do you have what I requested?"

"Can we speak in private?" asked Aunt Caris.

A distinct note of distress wove through her words. I fumbled with the buttons on the back of my borrowed dress, attempting to hurry the process. Granted, Melle and her family had just endured great upset. But what right did she have to make demands of Aunt Caris and cause her pain?

At last secured, I returned to the kitchen, but Aunt Caris and Melle were gone. The young mother awaited me, seated by the fire with her three little ones surrounding her.

She offered a hesitant smile. "How can I ever thank you for saving Essie?"

"Simply knowing she's well is sufficient." I smiled at the girl, and she gave me a shy grin in return. Only a reddish bruise on her cheek and still-damp curls, which coiled raven-dark around an impish face, attested to her fall.

"I suppose we'd best give introductions." She swept the hair from Essie's face. "I hope you'll call me Isuel."

I nodded. "If you'll call me Jessa. And Melle is your mother?"

"Yes. Auntie Aebbe is her aunt, and she'll ignore you if you dare address her by anything more formal."

Aside from the two young boys, there was a conspicuous and unusual lack of male presence in the house. But I dared not inquire and cause offense or dredge up heartache. Instead, I accepted the tea she offered, relishing its heat. "How lovely that she lives with you."

The ebb and fall of conversation in the background intensified, and then Melle's voice became high and distinct. "You have no choice but to help. If you don't get us out of here—"

"These things take time." Aunt Caris's strained tone sent me to my feet. "I'll need a fortnight at least to try—"

"A fortnight? Ha! By then, who knows what devastation we'll have suffered? You have four days."

Isuel fumbled with another teacup and dropped it. It shattered on the polished oak floor. While she cleaned it up, I wavered. Would Aunt Caris welcome or resent my intervention? She'd sought to keep the truth from me since the beginning, and if I interfered . . .

Their voices lowered again.

"I beg pardon," Isuel murmured. "Mother can be difficult at times. It's only that she fears so for us."

"What does she fear?"

Isuel glanced at her children, her lip caught between her teeth. "Jan and Daw, why don't you take Essie to sort the last of the apples? You may each have one."

When they'd left, she turned to me, still cradling the shards of broken cup in her palm. "This mill . . . there's been endless trouble since we purchased it. Some say the old miller cursed it, others say his girl Nelda bears the blame. After he passed, she wed a scoundrel who took everything, sold the mill, and abandoned her. They say the loss has driven her mad, and she seeks to reclaim her home by driving us out."

She tossed the remnants of the cup into the rubbish bin. "The mill seemed like a blessing in a time of trouble, small enough that we could run it ourselves with perhaps one or two hired hands, vital enough to the region to give us a good living. Mother knew it needed some repairs, thus the lower price, but had no idea the truth of the matter. If anyone had told her, I can't imagine she'd have purchased it . . . but now, it's too late. If we don't turn things around, we'll have nothing left."

A family of women and children cast out into the world without resources would land in the workhouse—or worse. I shifted on the hard wooden chair. "What sort of trouble have you experienced?"

"It started so small. One morning, we discovered the sheep pen had been left unlocked overnight. We lost several of the flock, but we thought perhaps it was an oversight or one of the children forgot." She swiped a cloth across the table, polishing the already-clean surface. "But then the barns flooded. Someone wrote in mud on the side: *Leave.* Afterward, some of our animals sickened, and a week later, five of our sheep somehow escaped the locked pen and were drowned in the millpond. Every time something else goes amiss, we find the word *leave* written in mud somewhere on the mill grounds."

I gripped the teacup, but its warmth no longer provided comfort. No wonder Mrs. Wilkins had suggested we stay clear and wanted the stratesman to arrest Nelda. "And you've seen no one?"

She shrank into herself. "Once, I saw some lights bobbing near the mill, but when I ran out, they were gone. No one was there. It's happened to Mother too, more than once. We had some items disappear . . . and now the sinkhole. I can't imagine how Nelda could have caused such a thing. She doesn't have the means to purchase alchemical devices, even were she so driven. Perhaps it's not related to the rest. Certainly, if today's incident stood alone, it would appear as a simple misfortune."

But as one of a greater sequence, it was troubling. I sipped my tea without tasting it. "I'm sorry you've experienced such difficulties. It must be frightening."

"Yes." Isuel lowered herself into the chair across from me. "I don't know what we're to do. To stay means to expose ourselves to danger. To leave . . . well, we have nowhere to go. And that's why I beg your forgiveness for Mother. She's not herself."

At the window, a graceful birch swayed in a gentle breeze, its placid motions a stark contrast to the dread clearly coiled within Isuel and the harsh murmur of discord between Aunt Caris and Melle.

Once again, that sense of Otherworldliness crept over me, like the pricking of a thousand tiny needles over my skin . . . and I wanted to flee. Instead, I gently placed my cup on its saucer, as if this were an ordinary house call, and prepared to seek answers.

But just then Aunt Caris stalked into the kitchen, her face flushed and green eyes vibrant as spring grass. "Come, Jessa. We've stayed long enough."

It was the nearest I'd ever heard her come to administering a direct cut.

Melle followed her into the room, displaying no emotion whatsoever. "It appears your clothes are still wet, Miss Jessa. You may as well take the ones you're wearing and return them later."

How did one respond in such a situation? I stammered my thanks, the tension between the two older women twisting my tongue. Ives was waiting by the door, and he sprang into action when Aunt Caris swept out.

I followed in her wake, rudderless and adrift. I'd thought Melle and Aunt Caris were friends, but their interactions indicated otherwise. So what had forced Aunt Caris to accept such ill treatment? The only logical explanation was some sort of extortion, but what could Melle possibly hold over her? The most scandalous thing Aunt Caris had ever done was to leave the house without a hat one day in a fit of abstraction, only to return moments later to properly attire herself. Yet Melle must have some means of exerting control.

If only Aunt Caris weren't so determined to hide the truth.

CHAPTER 4

On the trip back to the inn, Aunt Caris closed her eyes, shutting off conversation. But she did not sleep. Her breathing remained ragged and uneven, and damp gathered beneath her copper lashes.

I reached toward her, then let my hand fall back into my lap. She could scarcely send a clearer message that she wished to remain undisturbed. Her distance pricked like the spines of a thistle. I rubbed my chest. How could I condemn her for keeping her own counsel when I so often chose that course myself? But in this circumstance, reason failed to console. She didn't trust me with whatever troubled her, and worse, she held some sort of secret that caused her great pain.

Rather than risk upsetting her further, I collected the pencils and paper I'd scattered about the carriage in our rush to disembark and turned my attention to what little I knew about the situation. I couldn't shake the sensation that there was more involved in the disturbances at the mill than mere sabotage. What of the malicious laugh that had echoed through the mill yard?

I wished to forget, but it remained emblazoned on my mind. Did it indicate a malevolent spectator? If so, how had they concealed themselves, and why had no one else seemed to notice? Perhaps because there was nothing to notice. Perhaps my unchecked emotions had misled me once again, a good deal more grievously this time. But how could I force myself to feel nothing when a life was in danger? I smoothed a sheet of paper that had become crumpled and tucked it back into my satchel.

Somehow, I needed to persuade Aunt Caris to offer what assistance she could manage and then depart for Avons before she found herself inextricably entangled in the dangers at the mill—and whatever threat Melle held over her.

By the time we reached our rooms at the inn, Aunt Caris had regained her composure. "I must hurry to post a letter before luncheon. It won't take long, and I'm sure you'll want to tidy up and get into your own clothes before the meal."

Now I knew she was avoiding me. Like Ada and Ainslie, Aunt Caris preferred company wherever she went. Under normal circumstances, she would have waited for me to don proper attire, and we would have strolled to post the letter together, her chatter livening the walk. I adjusted the neckline of my borrowed gown. "I don't mind accompanying you. It won't take me long to change."

"No, dear." Aunt Caris slipped the letter into her reticule. "That won't be necessary."

Then she swept from the room.

Jade broke the ensuing silence with a fierce yowl from the bedchamber, where I'd confined her in our absence. I opened the door, and she stalked out, sniffing at my boots. The fur on the back of her neck rose, and she gave a dissatisfied growl. Perhaps she disliked the scent of mill-yard muck that clung to my shoes.

I reached down and picked her up, and she nuzzled my chin, as if assuring herself all was well.

While I examined her wounds and reapplied salve, I considered how to approach Aunt Caris upon her return. Tension wrapped around my chest like the coils of a fearsome serpent. However little I liked it, I could no longer avoid the issue.

I waited until dinner, when we were settled in our private dining room, with the fragrance of roasted meat and rich seasoning filling the air. The White Hart certainly didn't stint on meals, and if I weren't so nervous, I would have partaken with delight. But there could be no more delay.

"Aunt Caris, I couldn't help but overhear Melle demanding your assistance." I nibbled at some roast chicken, redolent with rosemary and sage. "And Isuel told me they've faced a great deal of trouble at the mill. What is it Melle hopes you'll do?"

She bit into a yeast roll and chewed an impossible number of times before finally offering an answer. "They want to leave, but have no way out. Dealing with the damages has cost far more than they expected, and though they've economized, they've run through their resources."

That explained why they had no cook, no nursemaid, not even a maid-of-all-work, unusual for the proprietors of such a business.

"No one will buy the mill now, even if this Nelda is arrested. There are too many rumors, too much fear. But if they abandon it, they'll land in the workhouse. Melle is strong. She might survive it. But the little ones and Aebbe . . . they wouldn't last long."

The notion stole all the savor from the meal. "What does she expect from you? Does she think you can press the stratesman to find the culprit? He appears to be investigating already."

"That's not what she wants." Aunt Caris laid down her fork,

its polished surface glinting silver. "There's no reason for you to trouble with this, dear. If I'd known the situation was so precarious, I'd never have brought you along."

"If it troubles you, it troubles me. And to think of those children with nowhere to go . . . of course we should do all we can." I touched her arm and found that she trembled slightly—with restrained emotion? "But what can we do? Would they consider a position in service or a shop? Could we help them find work?"

Aunt Caris pulled away. "No. Service positions might accept Melle and Isuel, but not Aebbe and the children. And Melle refuses to consider any sort of separation. I can't say I blame her. There's a mill near Middlebrook for sale. It's a great deal more costly than Dyott Mill, since it's closer to civilization. Melle preferred it originally but didn't have the finances to make the purchase, even once she'd sold off all that remained of their belongings after the deaths of her husband and son-in-law. But it's ready to offer a good livelihood. She wants me to buy it on their behalf and assist in their relocation. Later, as she is able, she'll repay me for the expense."

Later might well be never. And if it were a substantial sum, it would be beyond Aunt Caris's means. I poured a cup of tea. "How much does this other mill cost?"

She murmured an astounding amount, as if by speaking it in a whisper, she minimized its impossibility.

I gulped the tea, scalding my tongue. I struggled not to cough, and after a moment, I managed to clear my throat. "Such a figure . . . she can't possibly believe you could manage it."

Aunt Caris's inheritance from her parents remained locked in a trust until she wed—a fate unlikely at her age—and she lived on the small interest it generated and Father's provision.

Aunt Caris studied the floral pattern on the rim of her plate as if it were engraved with ancient runes. "I admit, I don't see a way, but I have to try."

How could she possibly acquire the funds? Even if Father could free up such a sum, he'd never agree to use it for strangers, not when three daughters required dowries and the estate must be maintained. Aunt Caris must have rejected the notion of approaching him out of hand, and I didn't blame her. It would have drawn unwanted attention to the entire expedition.

Nor did I have anything to offer. Even the small amount Mother had left us was held in trust. I had nothing to pawn either, aside from a simple pearl necklace, which befit our respectable but hardly lofty position in society. Even if I'd brought it with me, it would fetch only a tiny fraction of the required sum.

I traced the etching on my teacup. "Haven't you told Melle the truth? If this is her plan, it's doomed to fail."

"She refuses to accept it."

"Her acceptance or denial won't change reality." I clenched my linen napkin into a ball, then attempted to smooth the wrinkles. "If she would consider some other sort of position, there might be a way—"

"Don't you think I've tried to induce her to reconsider?" Aunt Caris set down her goblet with a thud. "There are things you can't possibly understand, Jessa. I'm doing this for your own good and that of your sisters also. Nothing matters more to me than to see you well-settled."

I'd never doubted she'd do anything for us, but how did the situation with Melle connect to us? I could only think of one way, confirming my earlier suspicions. "Is Melle attempting some sort of extortion?"

She drew back, and color surged into her face. "Are you suggesting I have some unsavory secret?"

"Of course not, Aunt Caris, but—"

"Then I'll hear no more of such wild suggestions."

I shrank from the displeasure bleeding through her words, and we continued the meal without further conversation. But hints of fear revealed themselves beneath the anger, in her unseeing stare and the pallor that crept across her cheeks as the flush subsided. As much as I longed for the truth, I couldn't bear to cause her further distress by prodding into whatever painful secret she clearly held.

Yet I couldn't refrain from speculation. Possibilities proliferated in my mind as rapidly as mint shoots in springtime, further souring the meal.

If her secret could impact our futures, it must be something that carried more than a hint of scandal. Try as I may, I couldn't imagine proper Aunt Caris drawing social censure or acting outside her expected role as a gentlewoman . . . unless it were for love.

Could that be the source of her secret? Had she perhaps fallen for an improper suitor? Maybe even risked it all and attempted elopement? No one in my family had ever so much as hinted at a romantic entanglement in her past, but it was possible.

Still, however shocking such an act might have been at the time, could it truly blight our prospects so many years later? Perhaps her fears for Ada, Ainslie, and me only represented her overprotective nature emerging. She championed our futures with great zeal, always seeking what she viewed as our best. I folded my napkin and placed it on the table.

Or might her secret resemble mine? Had she borne some sort of affliction, a taint in the blood? If so, she'd never signaled it by any outward act, but perhaps she was better at dissembling than I believed. But what could it be? She was in full possession of her faculties, so she couldn't be fae-touched. But perhaps she'd engaged with the Otherworld in some way in her girlhood that led her to dread such an accusation now? That would justify her fears of ruined prospects for me and my sisters.

Yet unless she confided in me, this was all conjecture.

Even though Aunt Caris donned a more cheerful demeanor following luncheon and insisted on a short exploration of Milburn, I could not shake my concerns. After we snuffed the candles for the evening, I wrapped myself in the bedclothes and stared at the ceiling, turning the new information over in my mind. Sleep held itself distant, so I quietly relit a candle and began to draw, my emotions pouring out in furious movements, dark lines, and deep shadows. The sinkhole took form on the page, then the mill grounds, the pall that hung over them etched into every line. At last spent, I set the image aside.

If Aunt Caris refused to leave without finding funds to purchase a livelihood and relocate an entire family, then we faced an impossible task. She had given everything for me, surrendered any opportunity of having a husband and children of her own to tend the three of us girls. I would give anything to help her—if only I could find a way out.

In the morning, Aunt Caris announced she needed to consult an official at the bank, which left me free to enact my plan. I would go back to Dyott Mill, ostensibly to restore the borrowed clothes and ask permission to do some sketching on the grounds, but in actuality to uncover what was happening there.

If I solved the mystery and the stratesman took the culprit into custody, then Melle and her family could make a home and living at the mill—and Aunt Caris would be free. I'd practiced gathering facts and uncovering answers within my own comfortable spheres, those of books and drawings, of plants and their properties, but this was another matter entirely. Still, once I stepped out the door, the brilliant spring sunshine lifted my spirits and made the daunting task feel more possible.

Aunt Caris required the carriage, but I welcomed the walk. Once beyond the town proper, the heady scent of alysbalm drifted on the breeze, lightening my heart. On foot, I admired more closely the wildflowers along the road, a smattering of vivid colors that heralded the triumphant return of spring. Their beauty sent a thrill through my soul.

As I neared the mill, gnarled oaks and towering elms overhung the lane, casting it into shadow. They swayed gently, beckoning me. And the vines banding the cage within began to fray. Since our arrival here and all the attendant upheaval, I couldn't rely on them as fully as I once had. Even with my efforts to strengthen them, they felt far too weak, too readily worn. So I brought another defensive mechanism to bear, fixing my gaze on the rocks and ruts of the road and reciting one of Mother's favorite poems. She'd dearly loved *The Ballad of Weston*, a tale of valiant fae warriors protecting the sun sylphs from the flame-birds that would steal their warmth, so much that she'd scribed it in her own personal copybook, claiming it evidence that not all fae were cruel. I worked to recall in exact detail the lofty language and intricate descriptions of the numerous verses, and so drove back the distracting sensations, until the soft sound of weeping broke my concentration.

I rounded a bend, and the slight woman I'd seen in the stratesman's shadow when we'd arrived in Milburn stumbled down the lane, her gown of muslin streaked with dirt and littered with forest debris. She clutched a ragged silk shawl around her shoulders, as though it could shield her from notice.

Nelda, Mrs. Wilkins had called her. Her palm dripped blood, and tears streaked her cheeks. For a moment, I remained rooted in place. If the townsfolk were to be believed, Nelda had brought a vengeful attack against Melle and her family. But the downcast lines of her body spoke of brokenness and distress, not malice.

"Nelda?" I hoped she wouldn't take offense at the use of her given name from a stranger. I hurried forward. "You're hurt. What happened?"

"I . . . I don't know." Nelda lifted her hand and watched as blood wept from it, one drop after another splatting against the dusty surface of the road. The wound cut deep.

Could Mrs. Wilkins have been right when she'd suggested madness? I shifted the bundle of clothes from one arm to the other. "Can I accompany you home and find someone to tend your injury?"

She laughed, a wild, off-key sound. "Home? I have no home."

"Then where are you staying?" I lowered my voice in an attempt to soothe her. "I'll help you there and fetch an herbalist, if it suits you."

"Staying? No one will house me. Not after what's happened at the mill." She jabbed toward the trees with her uninjured hand. "I stay in the forest. At least here, I'm close. Close to where home used to be."

I drew in a sharp breath. To live in the forest, this close to a Crossing? It was unthinkable. Otherkind might lurk anywhere, not to mention natural predators. Had the entire town truly forsaken her, simply because she'd wed the wrong man and he'd abandoned her? Or was there more that I missed? Society offered swift condemnation for those who failed to abide by its strictures, but other than a poor choice in a husband, what wrong had she done?

She swayed, and I rushed to steady her. "You can't stay out here. You need proper shelter and someone to look at your wound. Come with me into Milburn, and we'll find an herbalist."

"No, I can't." She backed away, every scrap of color leeching from already-pale features. "No one here wants to help. They'd only try to lock me up!"

Lock her up? Was the condemnation of the townsfolk truly so strong as to cross from indifference to active hostility? I recalled the scene at the inn upon our arrival, and I wavered. Perhaps she was right, but could I treat an injured woman? It was one thing to tend to Jade, but if I mismanaged Nelda's injury, the weight of guilt would be unbearable. I had no doubts about plants and their healing properties, but when it came to using them to assist people . . . no, my skills were best suited to creating an herbalism guide for others to consult. But this was no ordinary situation, and some care would be better than none.

I surveyed the roadside and the lavish profusion of life in its borders. Not far down the way was a small cluster of comfrey, and nearby grew a patch of yarrow, its tiny white flowers clustered above feathery leaves. Added to the basic supplies I'd brought to the inn to tend Jade, they would do. "Wait here."

When I crested the roadside embankment to harvest the yarrow, a ring of rust-brown toadstools caught my eye. They were the sort said to be favored by capsmen, diminutive fae who cast a potent lure over any who stepped within their circles, causing them to crave the toadstools and devour their poison, whereupon they fell dead within the circle, their bodies used as fuel for some perverse fae ritual. The gruesome legend was impossible to confirm, as any victims would never survive to tell their tale. Yet I gave the unpleasant fungus a wide berth, collecting yarrow as far from the outer rim of the ring as possible. The feathery leaves brushed my skin with a soothing touch.

Meanwhile, Nelda rocked back and forth, muttering. She appeared unaware of my presence, locked in some inner conflict. A chill wisped across the back of my neck, like ghostly fingers brushing my skin. What if she truly *was* mad, her condition sparked by grief or fae-touch? If so, she might be responsible for the attacks at the mill, with little awareness of the harm she caused. I approached her once more, and the sweet-spice scent of the yarrow permeated the air between us.

As if the fragrance reminded her of my presence, she clutched at me with the bony fingers of her uninjured hand, her gaze stricken, almost childlike. "What am I to do?"

A smattering of freckles stood stark against her colorless skin, and her pale amber eyes sank deep within their sockets, as though her trials had worn her to a weary shadow of herself. Perhaps she'd no involvement with the events at the mill after all. Regardless, to abandon her here in such a state was unthinkable. I eased closer. "Why don't you return to the inn with me?"

"Mr. Wilkins'd never allow it. He won't have me near. I offered to serve when my . . . when *he* left, but old Wilkins, he said no. No madwoman in his inn." Again the out-of-kilter laugh, high and slightly hysterical.

"I'm sure we can persuade him." Though I felt no such certainty, I steered her the way I'd come. I was a paying guest, and if I housed her in my room, maybe he'd be amenable.

"Why should you try?" She stopped in the center of the lane, tugged herself free. "No one keeps their word, no one cares. Not even Father did, not so long as I kept him well-fed and the cottage tended. So what do you truly want?"

My throat tightened. What a dreadful fate she'd endured—forsaken, rejected by all who should care, and viewed as an object of reproach. How could I leave her so? I extended my hand to her once more. "No one should suffer alone. I'd like to help. And I'd like to learn the truth."

"The truth . . ." She rubbed her head, then stared at the blood trickling down her wrist as if mesmerized. Had she encountered the fae? Had they stolen her memories of whatever happened to her?

Before any hope of answers, I needed to get her to safety. I wrapped my shawl around her gash to stop the bleeding and led her down the path. She shuffled alongside me, any will to resist vanished.

As we passed through town, whispers sprang up. I did my best to ignore them, but my face warmed under the scrutiny. Nelda's head bowed lower, strands of pale brown hair hanging limp over her eyes as she shuffled along.

We crossed into the courtyard of the White Hart and trod over the flagstones in demure silence, but hostile stares followed us nevertheless. Had I made a mistake in bringing Nelda here? If I didn't succeed in persuading Mr. Wilkins . . .

Once over the threshold, the moment of truth arrived. Mr. Wilkins stalked around the counter with the energy of a thunderstorm, attention fixed on Nelda. "What are you doing here? I told you if you came back, I'd have you removed by force."

Without allowing time for a response, he wheeled about and bellowed for a servant. "Dalton, get the stratesman here and quick."

Then he turned to me. "Miss Jessa, you're not to know, but you've been drawn into a dangerous situation. Just step away and let me handle the matter."

"Please, wait." I moved between him and Nelda. "I understand many think Nelda's responsible for what happened at Dyott Mill, but I found her wandering alone and injured. She needs aid."

"Aye, that may be. But the place for her is the madhouse." He rapped the countertop. "They know how to deal with her sort. If it's fae-touch that's confused her mind, they'll call the Vigil. If it's simply a case of wits addled by grief, they'll have her tended. Don't know why that stratesman hasn't sent her away yet."

Nelda flinched, and her head bowed even lower, signaling defeat.

The sight wrenched like a knife within. If Father hadn't protected me from speaking of what I sensed to the wrong people, hadn't warned me to lock my peculiarities away, would I have found myself like Nelda, alone and condemned by society? Her fate could well have been my own—might still, unless I could keep my affliction concealed. The knife twisted further.

Nelda didn't deserve to be handed over to the Vigil nor locked up in a madhouse, no more than I did, at least not without clear evidence of criminal activity.

"Wait, please." I fumbled for words that might influence Mr. Wilkins. "I don't think that's necessary, not yet. Let me tend her injury and give her a good meal. And then we can sort out where she's to go."

"I won't have her here, and that's flat. I've no mind to find my inn burned down around my ears."

"Of course, you need to protect the inn and those staying here, but I assure you I'll see that she stays out of trouble." The fountain behind us burbled merrily, almost mockingly. I knew so little of Nelda. Could I truly make such a promise? But what other choice did I have, except to abandon her to a harsh fate?

Mr. Wilkins was already shaking his head, but before he

issued another denial, I closed the distance between us. All my sorrow over her plight and determination to keep her from the Magistry—or worse, the Vigil—rose within me and flooded into my voice when I extended a final appeal. "Please, you've welcomed so many weary travelers over the years. Consider Nelda among those. She's alone and afraid and in need of our aid. Can't you extend your hospitality to include her, this once?"

He glanced between us, weighing, measuring. And at last, his dark eyes softened. "If you'll take responsibility for her whilst she's in the Hart, I suppose it'll be all right. But any oddities and she's out, you hear? And any damages will be tallied to your account."

"Of course."

His unexpected capitulation only traded one weight for another. To accept responsibility for a stranger . . . it wasn't a comfortable feeling. But I offered a smile despite my concerns. "Thank you."

Mr. Wilkins may have given consent, but Aunt Caris was another matter. She wouldn't approve, not of the risk nor of the possible entanglement in scandal—unless I appealed to her motherly instincts. Upon closer inspection, Nelda was no older than I. Perhaps the fact we were of an age with each other would incline Aunt Caris to sympathy.

I stumbled over the bottom step and forced my thoughts to the present. As we ascended the stairs, loud yowls from Jade descended to greet us. It was surprising Mr. Wilkins hadn't cast us out on her account—such a racket would hardly appeal to his guests. I'd better take her with me in the future. It wouldn't do to earn enmity, not when I'd brought Nelda here.

As soon as I walked through the door, Jade quieted, twining herself gingerly around my ankles. Her presence soothed me, the surprising constancy of her affection a comfort. She tapped her nose against my foot like a benediction and then curled up within her basket.

Nelda watched Jade with a wistful expression.

"Do you like cats?"

"I suppose. Da didn't hold with them, not even to keep the mice from the mill. He had a little dog, but he wasn't friendly." Her voice faded, and she stared into the distance.

"Please sit, so I can look at your injury." I crossed to my trunk, where I kept the supplies I'd brought to tend Jade. "I'd feel better if you'd let an herbalist—"

"No. No herbalists, not from here." She tugged at the shawl around her hand. Blood had already seeped through the layers.

"Then I'll do what I can." Quietly, I collected the necessary items and mixed a tincture with some wine for the pain. She drank it without complaint, and after giving it time to take effect, I examined the gash. It ran deep, but I cleaned and bound it the best I could.

All the while, she sat motionless. When I finished, she allowed her own shawl to fall from her bony shoulders and pool around her waist. The absence of the protection offered by the shawl revealed a small red birthmark only partly concealed by the sleeve of her gown. Superstition though it may be, such marks often caused rumors of Otherworldly influence to spread —small wonder she'd become a target for suspicion.

"Do you remember what happened to your hand?" I asked quietly.

She stared at it as though it belonged to someone else. "I just . . . wanted to see home again. I was careful, I protected myself. I wasn't like Da, who never took a caution. But I was at the river, and somehow, I . . . I'm not certain. I think I fell."

Something had shaken her, driven away clear recall. But it didn't appear she was able to offer more, so I rang the bell and requested luncheon, sufficient for three. I didn't know when Aunt Caris would return, but I suspected that in her absence, Nelda could do with the additional food.

I wasn't mistaken. She ate as though she hadn't enjoyed a proper meal in weeks, while I prodded at my pease soup with a carved spoon, releasing a minty aroma into the air. At last, I gathered my courage. "Nelda, I must know. Were you involved in what happened at Dyott Mill? The drownings, the destruction?"

She dropped her spoon with a clatter. "I would never—could never! I visit from time to time because I miss it so, but I didn't . . . I couldn't . . . please don't let them take me! They'll listen to you, maybe. Mr. Wilkins did."

By some chance of fate, he had, but I shrank from the notion of trying to sway a stratesman. "I'll do what I can."

As if the outburst had stolen her remaining strength, she drooped in her chair like a seedling too long without water. After the way of most inns, my bed had a trundle beneath it, so I pulled it out and suggested that she get some sleep.

I'd failed to make it to Dyott Mill and gather evidence that might extricate Aunt Caris and aid Melle's family, and I'd taken responsibility for a woman possibly mad. However, if Nelda were in my care, I might be able to uncover the truth of her innocence—or guilt.

If only Aunt Caris would agree. I rummaged through my sketching supplies, my fingers closing around a dulled pencil. My thoughts focused on the conflict to come, I picked up my penknife and began to sharpen its point.

Perhaps if I explained how I'd run across Nelda, how she was alone in the world . . . but Aunt Caris might easily counter by suggesting we get the stratesman involved. I slashed too hard with my penknife, shaving off a tremendous slice of cedar and nearly spoiling the pencil altogether. Better than my finger, at least.

Nelda appeared in the doorway. "Miss Jessa, I—"

Before she finished, a familiar step echoed down the hall. Blight and rot, I'd wanted time to prepare Aunt Caris for the idea before she set eyes on Nelda.

But it was too late.

CHAPTER 5

Aunt Caris entered the room with a flurry of complaints against unreasonable bankers and trustees. "If only they would consider—"

And then she spied Nelda. She was too much a lady to betray her shock, beyond the minute lift of a brow. She turned to me and spoke in a measured tone. "Jessa, what is the meaning of this?"

Her disapproval knotted my stomach. She hadn't spoken to me in such a manner since I'd transplanted a lady orchid into one of the Caldwell family vases. In my defense, I'd been only six years old, and the vases had been placed in the attic, where they'd become covered in dust and browned with age . . . but apparently they were still heirlooms not to be marred by soil and root.

I swallowed hard. However much I wished to please her, I was no longer a child, and I couldn't abandon Nelda, not after offering aid.

"Nelda, will you wait here?"

Body rigid, Nelda gave a tiny nod.

Jade roused from slumber to stretch and glare at Aunt Caris from slitted eyes. I willed her to remain quiet. If she launched into one of her bone-chilling yowls, I might give in to the impulse to flee the tension in the room. I straightened. "Aunt Caris, I can explain. If we could speak in your bedchamber . . ."

"Come along, then." Color high, Aunt Caris bustled into the bedchamber. The moment she swung the door shut, she went on the offensive. "Tell me I'm mistaken, and that's not the girl responsible for the destruction at the mill?"

"She's the one they believe responsible, yes, but—"

"Then by the Crossings, what is she doing here?" Aunt Caris fanned herself vigorously. "Haven't we trouble enough?"

I drew a deep breath. "I found her alone and injured, so I invited her to stay, just for a few days while we sort out matters with the mill."

Aunt Caris collapsed onto the nearest chair. "You invited her to *stay*?"

"Given the circumstances, you'd have done the same." I summed up what little I knew of Nelda, how she'd been abandoned without home or kin, and how I'd encountered her in the lane. I sank into the chair across from Aunt Caris. "Can we truly turn her away?"

The indignation ebbed from Aunt Caris. She opened the door a crack and peered at Nelda, who huddled on the divan, clutching her shawl about her once more and looking every bit a forlorn child. She sighed. "Perhaps not. But if you advocate for her and you're wrong, you may receive some blame for her actions. It's a risk, and if your father knew I let you take it, he'd be furious."

"The risk is minor, as long as we attend her. If we must leave her behind, we can ask Ives to keep watch over her. It will be a safeguard for us all." I leaned forward, bracing on my elbows. "If she's under observation, then maybe the stratesman will give his attention to finding the true culprit."

"You're so certain she's innocent, my dear?"

"I am."

"Well, I suppose she may stay, for now." Her tone still held doubt, but I'd won the consent I needed.

We passed a quiet night, and I began to hope my decision to take in Nelda would cause no more difficulties. Over breakfast, Aunt Caris announced her intention to travel to the nearest town to speak with a different lender. During the meal, she softened further toward Nelda, and by the time we finished, she extended an invitation to her.

"Come with me," she said. "The trip will take a full day, and it'll do you good to be away from Milburn for a bit."

Though hesitant, Nelda agreed, which left me free to return to the mill. Aunt Caris instructed her to remain in our rooms until the carriage was ready, after which she'd send Ives to fetch her.

I gathered my reticule, sketching supplies, and hat. Evidently, Jade noticed my preparations for departure, for she tangled around my legs, protesting loudly. Though she offered a clear signal of her desire to accompany me, I couldn't haul her all the way to the mill. She batted at the hem of my skirt in further petition. Perhaps I might hire a carriage?

I lifted her from the floor, and she clambered up to drape herself over my shoulders like an enormous stole, her fur tickling my neck. The two of us trailed Aunt Caris down the stairs. If Jade had healed enough to climb to my shoulders with no apparent discomfort, maybe she could simply walk alongside me. But cats were not known for constancy of companionship, and if she lost herself in the forest, I'd worry endlessly over her fate. Better to hire a curricle from the White Hart's stable and have done with it.

But before I could carry out my plan, Ives approached Aunt Caris with his hat in his hands. He twisted it uncomfortably. "Begging your pardon, Miss Caldwell, but I can't find Simms anywhere. We parted after supping yesterday, and I've not seen him since."

"Oh heavens." Aunt Caris stopped midmotion. "Did he confide his plans in you?"

"No, Miss Caldwell, nary a word."

"It's most unlike him." The color leeched from her face.

I stepped toward Ives. "Has Simms frequented any of the local establishments since our arrival?"

"Not that I know. The common room here provides pleasant enough occupation in our off hours. He's gone strolling a time or two but never spoke much of it."

"And you've asked about the inn?" I peered over his shoulder as if I might catch a glimpse of Simms's darkly-thatched head.

"Aye, miss. None of the servants have seen him either."

"Oh, this is dreadful." Aunt Caris clutched at her chest. "How can he have simply vanished?"

As if drawn by the note of distress in her voice, Mr. Wilkins approached. "What's all this? May I offer assistance?"

Ives repeated himself, and Mr. Wilkins drummed his fingers against his leg as he listened. When Ives concluded his account, Mr. Wilkins dispatched a manservant to scour the grounds. "I'm certain he'll turn up soon, and none the worse for wear."

But as time dragged on, Aunt Caris grew increasingly restive. "What if Simms has been led astray by a will-o'-the-wisp and lured too near the Crossing? Or suffered some other dreadful fate?"

Her leap to worry contradicted her usual cheery nature. I

extended my hand toward her, and she clasped it as though I'd offered her an invaluable treasure.

"Now, Miss Caldwell, don't worry yet." Mr. Wilkins pushed back the brim of his hat. "It's more likely he had a drop too much last night and is sleeping it off somewhere. Never you fear, we'll find him."

But his manservant could find no more trace of him than Ives. Mr. Wilkins dispatched the man to seek Simms elsewhere, then summoned Mrs. Wilkins. Once apprised of the situation, she offered her own reassurances to Aunt Caris, followed by the promise of a soothing cup of tea in her private sitting room. Aunt Caris accepted with thanks, but I declined.

I didn't think I could face the steady stream of conversation Mrs. Wilkins was sure to offer—I yearned for the peace and solitude that had been sorely lacking since our departure from Avons. So after I informed Nelda of the situation, I sought the garden behind the inn.

She'd adamantly refused to accompany me, insisting her needlework would provide ample occupation, and I couldn't help but feel relief. I needed the quiet to clear my thoughts, and the garden beckoned.

Across an open expanse, it unfolded in neat boxes with stone pavers creating paths between. Clearly, it had been designed for function, not form, yet beauty thrived nevertheless in the pleasing juxtaposition of texture and color. A wide variety of common herbs and fruiting plants flourished, as well as a few more unusual species—pale pink lamb's tongue, rough and nubbly; darkly elegant greensward, smooth and sharp-edged; and coppery-bright cobblescaw, broad and spreading.

Jade sprang from my shoulders and began to investigate beneath sprawling grape vines, and I meandered after her. As the sound of voices from the courtyard faded, sprightly whispers swirled round me, composing an inviting song of renewal and restoration. Instinctively, I sought to strengthen my inner cage, then hesitated. The melody spoke of regeneration—precisely what I required to heal Ainslie's scar.

Perhaps I could allow myself to listen for just a moment . . .

I spun in place, seeking the source of the song. When I turned westward, it strengthened, and I followed the sound. Surely I could bolster the cage within once I found what I sought.

Beneath the thick boxwoods that formed the boundary of the garden, I located the source of the song—singular plants, translucent white in stem, leaf, and bloom. Their blossoms resembled an inverted pipe, with a single dark-red splotch in the underside of the bowl.

I removed one glove and allowed myself to touch the bloom. Soft and sure came a name: *amelior*. The prickling sense of Other lurking in Milburn surged around me, and I staggered back. What was happening to me? Even on the most trying of days, I'd never imagined a plant bespeaking its own name, nor evoking a feeling so strong.

I distanced myself from the ghostly plants, pressing my fingers to my suddenly throbbing temples. One by one, I strengthened the vines within.

And nothing changed.

The whispers still swirled around me; the air still pinpricked against my skin with the discomfiting sensation of Other. I froze in place as if rooted there myself, and my heart drummed against my stays.

What now?

Jade bounded to my side and pressed herself against me, her presence warm and tangible in contrast to the ethereal whispers. Then she stood on her hind legs and braced herself against my skirts. Her familiar *mrow* broke the power of the murmured melody.

With effort, I forced my feet to move. I staggered back one step, two, increasing the distance between myself and the amelior.

Jade kept pace with me, trilling encouragement.

This would work; it must. I closed my eyes and turned my attention inward, adding to my cage until I could hear nothing beyond the chatter in the courtyard and the soft rustle of wind in the leaves.

I lifted Jade once more, and she nuzzled my chin. Gradually, my breathing evened, and I turned back to the inn. I should never have allowed the whispers entrance, not even for a moment. Father had warned me about self-governance, but I'd grown careless.

Perhaps if I resumed every precaution, I could still use them to help Ainslie. If the plant carried some of the Otherworldly properties of the nearby Crossing, perhaps that's what had caused the unusual surge of sensation. And perhaps that property would enable me to create a successful salve this time. Though I'd rather never see the amelior again, I'd ask Mrs. Wilkins if she minded me transplanting a few of them into the collections basket I'd brought so I might take them home and continue experimenting on a salve for Ainslie's scar.

It was worth the risk to offer Ainslie aid, but I would exercise great care working with it. I certainly had no intention of touching it ungloved again.

I drew Jade closer. The garden no longer felt welcoming, not when it carried such threats. However little I might desire the company of others, it was time I returned to the inn and Aunt Caris. And past time we found a way to go home—before Milburn exerted its influence in a way I could not escape.

It was nearly noon before Mr. Wilkins rejoined us, our coachman stumbling after him into the common room where we now waited.

"Seems my guess about your man wasn't far from the mark, only it's not his fault. It appears some of the local lads thought it'd be good sport to offer him some frostwine." Mr. Wilkins's mouth pinched. "Mr. Butterwick makes it from the frost grapes that grow by the Crossings. Only fools dare tread there, let alone brew their ill-gotten goods."

"Oh my." Aunt Caris looked between the two men. "I do hope you're unharmed, Simms."

"I feel as though I've been dragged behind my own team, but it's naught that'll linger." He spoke thickly, as though the Crossing-influenced potion still dried his tongue. "Wilkins says I'll be my old self, iffen I let him take care of me."

"Aye, I've treated many an overindulgence in my day. Golda keeps a store of infusions on hand that'll sort a man." He clapped Simms on the back, nearly knocking him over. "A sip or two of frostwine is enough to fell a grown man, and your driver here had a sight more than that, on account of the dare and not knowing what he took. I'll see him set to rights."

"Thank you, Mr. Wilkins." The tense set of Aunt Caris's shoulders relaxed. "Your aid in this matter is most appreciated."

"It's only my duty, Miss Caldwell." Mr. Wilkins maintained a steadying hand on Simms. "The conduct of the lads reflects poorly on Milburn, but I hope you won't take too dim a view of us. If you've still a mind to go out, I'll send Topper to drive you, no extra charge."

"How very kind of you," Aunt Caris said. "But my business

will take a full day, and I don't like the look of those clouds. I believe we'll stay nearby this afternoon."

The urgency of my earlier encounter nearly prompted me to protest, but I did not wish to draw questions from Aunt Caris. She believed I intended nothing but a jaunt around Milburn, and it wouldn't do to indicate otherwise.

"As it pleases you, Miss Caldwell."

Then Mr. Wilkins ushered Simms back to the servant's quarters, and we went back to our rooms to take luncheon with Nelda. As it turned out, Aunt Caris was correct about the foreboding clouds, for we soon had a downpour, and she insisted we remain indoors all that interminable day. I only hoped the delay would do no harm.

CHAPTER 6

Following the downpour, morning dawned bright and clear, full of fresh promise. After I saw Nelda and Aunt Caris off with a fully recovered Simms, I hired a curricle from the White Hart's stable as I'd planned the day prior. Before Jade and I departed Milburn to call upon Melle and Isuel, I stopped in a sweetshop near the inn to purchase a small box of marzipan as a gift for the children. Jade sniffed it, then perched beside me on the seat of the curricle, surveying the row of shops as we passed by.

The early sun was so glorious that once I was beyond the outskirts of the town, I slid my hat down to let it bathe my face. Dappled light and shadow played across the horses' backs as I drove through the narrow, forest-lined stretch of the road where I'd met Nelda before.

Blessedly, none of the plants murmured. My determined good cheer and fortification of my inner cage held the boundary secure for now. As we passed, the trees rustled, an ordinary sort of rustle, carrying neither word nor song.

Except there was no reason for their movement. No birds fluttered through their limbs, no breeze stirred the air.

A tingle of unease shot down my spine.

Was someone hiding among them? And if so, were they mortal or fae? Friend or foe? I touched the ward-pendant Aunt Caris had purchased for me prior to our departure. Never mind that no one knew the extent of their effectiveness against Otherkind, it provided a sense of safety. I hoped it wouldn't be proven false.

At once, Jade sat upright, intensely alert, her pupils dilated.

"What do you see?"

She rumbled deep in her chest, an ominous sound, and I offered a gentle pat, meant to reassure, even as my mind conjured all sorts of lurkers in the shadows, vivid images drawn from fae lore. Many Otherkind favored the forests, from the dangerously alluring tree nymphs to the fierce, bestial wildings of the wood. Would any of these sylvan fae venture beyond the Crossing to stalk Milburn in broad daylight? Certainly the townsfolk appeared to believe the greatest danger lurked at night, but how had they drawn those conclusions?

The leaves of the tallest oak shivered, and I could almost imagine the Green Man peering through the foliage, his hair and beard of riotous leaves, his emerald eyes glinting as he sought to send growth beyond the forest, rooting new trees over town and field alike.

I tightened my hold on the reins. Perhaps I should not have ventured beyond the town borders alone. But it was more probable that I permitted my imagination too wide a scope. If by chance some sort of fae creature did haunt the woods, my best hope was to act as natural as possible. If I drew their interest or appeared an easy, entertaining target, I would endanger Jade and myself. So I would keep calm, maintain a steady pace, and trust my ward-pendant was reliable.

Another rumble came from Jade. She kept vigil until we passed a gnarled stand of elms and reached a more open stretch of the road, and then she calmed, nestling in my lap.

My own disquiet eased. Most likely, we'd been threatened by nothing more than a fox or some other woodland creature, but I was relieved to be out from beneath the deep shadows of the trees nevertheless. With effort, I turned my thoughts from hidden foes to the situation at the mill.

Aside from Nelda, who would have an interest in seeing Melle and her family chased away? As a stranger in Milburn, I couldn't venture a guess, but perhaps Isuel would provide names. She seemed more willing to speak than Melle.

At last, Dyott Mill came into view. I relaxed my grip on the reins and prepared to disembark. Before I moved, Jade climbed onto my shoulders once more, the fur on her neck standing on end. Evidently, she didn't share my relief at our arrival.

When I attempted to dislodge her, she allowed her weight to go limp, and my efforts ended in failure. I surrendered with a sigh and climbed down from the curricle, nearly unbalanced by the cumbersome load. I stroked her head. "It's fortunate for you that you're such good company, else I might not keep lugging you along."

She gave a purr of satisfaction, and I smiled. We picked our way carefully around the sinkhole, which glinted darkly. I averted my eyes from its depths and attended instead to the whitewashed cottage ahead, made cheery by a bright blue door and flowers planted along its front.

When I knocked, Isuel answered the door, her demure composure a stark contrast to our prior encounter. "Good morning, Miss Jessa." Her gaze immediately trailed to Jade. "I see you've brought your . . ."

Small wonder she had difficulty placing Jade's bulky frame as that of a cat. Certainly, she bore little resemblance to the tidy balls of fluff favored by most ladies. "My cat. Forgive me, but she's recovering from some injuries, and I didn't want to leave her alone at the inn all day. I hope you don't mind. I can return her to the curricle, if you prefer."

Jade prodded my neck with a claw, as if to signal her protest.

"She's more than welcome, and so are you." Isuel stepped back to let me enter. "I'd hoped we'd have another chance to talk."

"I've brought back the clothes you so kindly lent me." I lifted the bundle. "They've been cleaned, of course."

Essie pattered down the hall and offered me a shy smile. "Can I pet the cat? Please?"

Again the jabbing claw of protest.

"I can't answer for her temperament at the moment." Or ever, for though she'd been an excellent companion to me, she bristled when anyone else attempted to draw near and had even snarled at Eda this morning when she'd dared to move Jade's basket while cleaning our rooms. "Maybe another time."

Her face fell slightly, but she didn't protest.

I rummaged in my reticule to withdraw the marzipan, and the tantalizing almond aroma wafted into the air. "But I brought this for you and your brothers, if your mother approves."

"Of course I do," Isuel said.

Essie's shy smile became a full grin, and she bounded away, feet thudding back down the hall. "Jan, Daw! Look here."

"You've certainly brightened their day." Isuel gazed after her daughter with a soft, wistful expression. Then she beckoned me onward. "Won't you have some tea?"

"That would be lovely."

As I followed her down the hall, she called over her shoulder, "I'm glad you arrived without incident. Mother encountered a young cowherd in the lane this morning who said they'd lost several cattle to boggarts in the night. Evidently, he failed to maintain the wards properly."

I considered again how Jade had bristled at the rustling of the leaves. My ward-pendant hung heavy around my neck. "I . . . I'm grateful as well. Are such incursions frequent?"

"Enough that the townsfolk appear to accept it as a fact of life. I'm not certain I shall ever grow accustomed to it, but we've adopted all the precautions recommended to us and hope for the best."

Once in the kitchen, I perched on a spindled chair and coaxed Jade into my lap. In Avons, receiving a tea prepared by the mistress of the home would have been unthinkable. Given how Isuel flushed as she assembled the tea things, I suspected it might be so here as well. Once or twice, I thought she might speak, but she kept silent. Perhaps she felt the awkwardness of the situation as keenly as I.

I prodded myself to action. Small talk didn't come readily to me, but I managed to make some inconsequential remarks about her children and the lovely weather, the sort of polite chatter Aunt Caris and my sisters had drilled into me. *No, don't ask what they think of the Crossings theory. No, don't speak of the latest manuscript you've read. Simply inquire after the health of their family and comment on the weather . . . or perhaps the decor.*

And though I felt like I trudged up a muddy hill in a rainstorm, the idle conversation worked. Isuel relaxed, sat across from me, and poured out for us.

I sipped the tea, then chose my words with care. "I've been considering what you shared about the troubles you've experienced at the mill. I know you said many believe Nelda responsible, but I'd like to hear what you think."

Isuel's mouth twisted. "I think some townsfolk take pleasure in our misfortune. We're outsiders. And most don't think women should attempt to run a mill, even though Mama grew up a miller's daughter before she wed a merchant."

Would such prejudice motivate someone to sabotage Melle? Jade shifted, and I released my grip on her. "Has anyone been particularly outspoken against Melle's purchase?"

"Lord Ackerley." A flush spread up her neck and unfurled across her cheeks. "He owns one of the two large estates adjoining Milburn, and he's made his views quite plain. He carries influence, and he's swayed many. The village baker said he'd refuse to have us mill his flour, even if we do get it up and running."

I murmured condolences.

Her face had lost its usual dreamy expression, becoming tight with suppressed emotion. "What does it harm them if we succeed?"

"I'm sorry you've faced such opposition. If the baker has any sense, he'll soon change his views, given the decreased expense of using a local miller. But I suppose it's a moot point until the mill is repaired." I stirred a smidgen of milk into my tea to soften the flavor. "Were there others interested in purchasing it?"

"I'm not sure. Mother handles all such things, and well, she hasn't been talkative lately."

"And she doesn't want us to talk either." Aebbe wandered into the room. How long had she been listening?

Her wrinkled mouth stretched into a grimace. "I say it's time for truth. No more secrets."

Isuel blanched. "Auntie, I hardly imagine Jessa wants to hear—"

"Aye, she does." Aebbe studied me and nodded. "Else why would she be asking?"

I looked between them. I risked offending Isuel if I pressed, but if Aebbe had information . . . I set down my cup. "What do you know?"

"Auntie, I'm afraid I must insist." Isuel's voice firmed. "We don't need to be spreading wild rumors, not when we're newcomers here. The stratesman will find any evidence to be found—best leave it to him."

"Can't hush up truth, child."

The door banged open, and Melle entered. With only a curt nod to acknowledge my presence, she stepped in front of Aebbe. "Auntie, I need your aid."

Aebbe muttered a protest.

But Melle ignored her. She wrapped an arm around Aebbe's shoulders and steered her into the depths of the house.

I stared after them. Blight and rot, what was happening here?

Isuel gave a strained laugh. "I must apologize. All that's happened, it's been difficult for Auntie. She's gotten a ridiculous notion stuck in her head . . . but it has no bearing on our situation. If it did, you can be sure we would have informed the stratesman."

"Of course." But I no longer felt any certainty.

Isuel fidgeted, tucking a strand of dark hair behind her ear. "If you will excuse me, I need to check on the children."

"Certainly." I stood, Jade in my arms, and followed Isuel back to the entryway.

When the blue door shut firmly behind me, I lingered a moment on the stone step. What did Aebbe want to share? Had she confided in the stratesman or been hushed by her family?

And why would Melle and Isuel keep a secret that might lead to their ruin?

Unless they feared retribution from those in power if they spoke out. Every place people dwelt, from the smallest hamlet to the largest city, had its power-holders, those who exercised their will and influence over others, often without scruple. If Melle had truly run afoul of an influential citizen, then she operated under a deep disadvantage.

In the distance, the river churned relentlessly over the mill wheel, and Jade glared in its direction, growling low.

"Yes, I know, you don't like it here. We're going."

I climbed back into the curricle with Jade and lifted the reins.

Somehow, I needed to find evidence on the individual behind the sabotage at the mill—and quickly. That meant I'd have to pay calls, make small talk, and ask questions under pretense.

I'd rather harvest nettles.

CHAPTER 7

Several hours later, after returning to partake of luncheon at the inn, I stood before the door of the town haberdashery. If Milburn bore any similarity to Upper Northlea, the village nearest our country estate, the haberdashery would be an excellent place to glean gossip and gain insight into Milburn society. I gripped the battered hat I'd worn when I plunged into the sinkhole—my excuse for visiting the shop—crumpling it further.

Oh, I wished for Ada and Ainslie, for their enthusiasm and social grace to carry me onward and smooth over any awkward moments. But they were not here, and I *could* do this. I could discover the truth and help those I loved, but not if I dithered on the doorstep. I'd long known the thrill of uncovering answers and making connections, that glorious moment where one understood *why* or *how* or *what truly happened* and all sorts of delightful and intriguing possibilities coalesced into insight and knowledge.

If I treated this as simply another journey of discovery—like when I examined the properties of one unusual herb combined with another, or explored why alchemical knowledge vanished and what sparked the process of rediscovery, or puzzled together pieces of some antiquity with Ibbie—then perhaps it would bolster my courage. Never mind that the stakes in this case meant life and livelihood, rather than the satisfaction of curiosity.

I grasped the iron knob, and it sent an unpleasant chill through my fingers. It was bad enough to feel a peculiar sensation of Other in the land and that which grew from it, but now inanimate objects? What would happen if I couldn't find the saboteur, if we must prolong our stay? Would I lose my ability to control these sensations altogether? The chill traveled bone-deep.

I thrust the door inward and stumbled over the threshold into an immaculate space that smelled of polished wood and beeswax. Damaged hat in hand, I collected myself and strolled over to a stand of spooled ribbons, arranged by color.

A portly gentleman beamed from behind the counter. "Can I help you, miss?"

"Are you Mr. Wybert?" Considering the sign outside proclaimed this *Wybert Haberdashery*, it was a safe assumption, though an awkward opening remark. I restrained a wince.

"Indeed I am." He bowed affably. "And you must be new in town."

"Yes, this is my first visit to Milburn." I compared two shades of ribbon to the water-stained remnants on my hat. "My aunt is visiting a friend, and I accompanied her to sketch some of the lovely scenery here."

"Aye, we have views in abundance. If you want beauty, you've come to the right place." He adjusted wire-rimmed glasses over his bulbous nose. "Have you visited the hilltop ruins? Every artist who ventures here makes their way there sooner or later."

"I'm afraid I've done very little exploring so far, but I'll have to add that to my list."

"The Hollace and Ackerley estates are also a sight to behold. Their gardens are renowned, particularly the Ackerley's. Something about the Morven Crossing nearby does wonders for growing things."

Ackerley—as in Lord Ackerley? I fingered a broad periwinkle-blue ribbon. "Would they welcome visitors?"

A tall brunette girl swept out from the back room, her movements lithe as a lily swaying in a summer breeze. "The Hollaces welcome everyone—they practice hospitality as though it were their religion. But to call on the Ackerleys, you must be the right sort."

I caught my hand on the sharp edge of the rack and pulled in a breath. A gentlewoman with no title and only a small, obscure family estate was unlikely to qualify as the right sort. But I had to try.

"Mayla." Mr. Wybert—her father?—frowned at her. "You know Lord and Lady Ackerley are most generous patrons to our shop, indeed, to the whole town."

Her lips parted in what appeared more a grimace than a smile. "Certainly they are. They never pass up an opportunity to act with generosity in full view of the appreciative public."

"I'm certain their efforts are . . . welcome," I murmured. "I'd dearly love to see their gardens, if they would allow it. Where can I find them?"

Mr. Wybert launched into a detailed explanation of how to locate the Hollace and Ackerley estates, one located to the east and the other to the west of Milburn proper, complete with a litany of landmarks to follow. His flow of information only halted when a small bell chimed behind me, and an elderly woman with a gown in the unrelieved black of mourning tottered into the haberdashery.

Mr. Wybert hurried to help her across the room. "Miss Hildred, what can we do for you today?"

While they conversed about the best replacement for her favorite pair of gloves, Mayla leaned closer to me. "If you pay a call at Ackerley House, be sure to stay away from Lord Ackerley."

"Why?"

"He's very . . . fond of women." She seemed like she might say more, but her father glanced our direction, and she turned to examine the display. "Have you seen the picot-edged ribbon? We just received a supply a few days ago. The sapphire would complement your hat nicely—and it nearly matches your eyes, though of course they're much a richer shade."

She was a skilled saleswoman, weaving compliments with her recommendations, even praising my unruly dark curls, and she kept up her patter until I completed my purchase. When I left the shop, I tucked the larger-than-planned bundle beneath my arm, my mind humming with possibilities and questions.

But before I'd taken more than a step or two down the lane, Mayla came dashing after me. "Do you truly mean to go to Ackerley House?"

"Yes, it sounds like it would be a pleasant excursion." I couldn't confess I intended to gather information, so I hoped my earlier excuses were sufficient.

"Will your aunt be accompanying you?"

"She has business in Harbury today, so I intended to hire a curricle from the White Hart and go on my own."

"I see." She tucked her chin. "In that case, will you allow me to accompany you? I need to have a word with Lady Ackerley's housekeeper—we've had a delay with her order of material for the housemaids' aprons, and she'll expect a report in person."

How could I possibly decline? Never mind my lack of desire for company, Mayla knew Milburn and its inhabitants. If she would continue to speak her mind, she could shed additional light on the situation at the mill. I clutched the bundle tighter. "Thank you, that's very kind of you."

"Don't mention it. I'd no more send an unwary visitor to Ackerley House than cast them into a Crossing." She snapped out the shawl draped over her arm and wrapped it about her shoulders.

As we passed through the town, Mayla offered informative— and at times sharp—commentary on the shops and individuals we passed. Through her words, Milburn became more *real* to me, peopled with individuals of foibles and follies just like the rest of the kingdom. But none aside from Lord Ackerley leapt out as having a desire to remove Melle from the mill.

Once we entered the courtyard of the White Hart, one of the stable hands leapt to fetch a curricle for us, and in short order, we departed. If the Ackerleys cared about appearances, then presenting myself on foot would give an unfavorable impression, and if I was to gather information as I intended, I needed this visit to be a success.

As we drove away, I glanced back at the inn. Exploring the Ackerley estate would take most of the afternoon, assuming they granted us permission. I hoped Jade wouldn't rouse and create a disturbance before my return. After our trip to the mill this morning, her deepest gash had looked irritated, so with much sweet talk and an ample portion of valerian root, I'd induced her to rest in her basket and left her to sleep. She had food, water, and everything else she might need, but even so, it would be best to hurry.

Not far past the outskirts of Milburn, Mayla directed me onto a long, elm-lined lane. The boundary stones on either side bore the Ackerley name and family crest, and the drive led to a towering graystone house with iron-edged windows and doors, all rigid lines and unyielding angles, not a single beckoning curve in sight. However, landscaping in a glorious array of colors softened the exterior and drew the eye away from the stark lines of the manor to the stately trees and elegant gardens.

"I'll go round to the servant's entrance," Mayla said. "It shouldn't take me more than a moment or two—Infinite knows I'm not inclined to linger for a tongue-lashing about matters outside my control. You'll find me here at the curricle when you return, and if you're able to gain permission to view the grounds, I'll accompany you."

"Thank you."

After securing the curricle, I made my way to the front entrance. Tremendous gas lamps loomed on either side of the door, a rarity in an edgetown given the expense required for their procurement and maintenance outside of the city. Even the door knocker, an imposing draconic form with glittering jeweled eyes, bespoke a desire to impress. Suddenly, I wished I'd accompanied Mayla to the servant's quarters . . . but that would get me nowhere. So I reached for the dragon and brought its head crashing down.

A moment later, a dashing footman pulled open the iron-hinged doors and offered a greeting.

"Good afternoon." I presented him with my card. "I'd hoped to tour the gardens today."

"You'll have to ask Lady Ackerley," he said.

I'd apply to Lady Ackerley for permission, not the house-keeper? The lady of the house could give me additional under-standing of the family, which was fortunate, but she'd almost certainly subject me to greater scrutiny than a servant would. I drew myself up to my full, albeit scant, height. "Very well."

"If you'll wait here." He vanished into the depths of the house, presumably to see if Lady Ackerley would receive me. At least I'd arrived within normal calling hours, so I hoped that would work in my favor.

When he returned, he gave a slight bow. "Follow me, miss."

He ushered me through gaslit corridors into a large morning room, papered with a floral print and adorned with gilt-edged portraits and ornate ceramics, where he announced me to Lady Ackerley.

An imperious woman glided toward me. Her silvery hair swept upward in a towering profusion of curls, and like the petals of an incurve chrysanthemum, the ringlets swirled toward a glittering diamond comb which secured the whole elaborate concoction. A heavy gold-and-emerald necklace looped round her neck, and the stiff lines of her gown rustled as she moved.

Once near enough, she examined me as one might an insect under a microlens. "What brings you here?"

I lowered into a deep curtsey. "I'm sorry to trouble you, but I learned from Mr. Wybert at the haberdashery that you have the most magnificent gardens in the region. I hoped you'd permit me to tour your grounds and perhaps attempt to sketch them."

Her mouth tightened, and I sensed she was about to dismiss me as beneath notice, so I quickly added, "He mentioned the Hollace gardens as well, but I prefer to view the best, when possible."

"Then you were right to come here. Lady Hollace has only created a pale imitation of our gardens." She gave a magnanimous nod. "Yes, you may explore, but I'm afraid I can't spare a servant to take you around. They're needed to prepare for our dinner party."

"Of course. You've been more than generous to see me and grant your permission." I was laying it on a bit thick, but it had the desired impact.

She thawed slightly and lifted a golden quizzing glass to study me further. "You've called alone?"

Butterflies swirled in my stomach. It was time to mention the mill, and I couldn't predict how she'd react. "I'm afraid so. I traveled with my aunt, but she's occupied this morning helping a friend—Mrs. Hopkins of Dyott Mill."

"Dyott Mill?" Her gray eyes narrowed. "A young woman shouldn't allow herself to be tainted by unsavory companions, not even when prompted by a relative. No, I won't have it. You should distance yourself."

She spoke as one accustomed to having her slightest whim gratified, and given I still needed her goodwill, I clenched my hands in my lap and pretended to consider her statement. "Tainted, my lady?"

"By the strong-minded woman who lives there. Lord Ackerley says the whole situation is a disgrace, and I must say I agree." She sniffed. "Running the mill should have been left to the landowners of the region, not a newcomer—and certainly not a woman."

"A landowner familiar with the needs of Milburn would be well-suited to the task." Warmth spiraled up my chest to my neck, but I kept my tone neutral, fighting down the urge to defend Melle. "Perhaps Lord Ackerley might consider acquiring it?"

"Perhaps at one time he might have considered purchasing it, but now he has no interest. Whatever the trouble there, we'll not invite it onto our lands."

I tilted my head. "Then you believe the mill cursed? I've heard rumors, and of course, I'm concerned for my aunt."

"You're right to be concerned." She tapped her quizzing glass on the arm of her chair. "Edgetowns hold dangers you city-dwellers cannot fathom. As I said before, I suggest you and your aunt remove yourselves from any connection with the mill at once."

If Lord Ackerley believed the mill was a source of danger or carried some curse and therefore sought to avoid it, why protest Melle's involvement? Its success would aid the economic health of the whole region, and its purchase by an outsider would mean any associated risks wouldn't touch the Ackerley family.

Was it simply that a woman running the mill would disrupt the social order Lord and Lady Ackerley desired to maintain in Milburn? Was he displeased that he'd not been able to dictate the sort of individual who purchased the mill, even though he'd no desire for it himself?

Or was his motive monetary? Might he intend to build his own mill after the failure of the current one? An estate of this size and extravagance required a great deal to maintain. If he were to build a new mill with the most up-to-date methodology, it would run with greater efficiency and thereby earn its keeper more. His property adjoined the river, so it was feasible, and if he had the finances to invest, he could quickly turn a profit—as long as there wasn't another mill in town.

Before I could ask one of the multitude of questions simmering, the footman returned to the room. "Your sister is here, Lady Ackerley."

With that, she dismissed me with one more reminder to keep myself and my aunt far away from the mill. I'd received far more of her attention than I expected, and that only because she'd enjoyed the role of gracious lady lecturing an impressionable girl. I slipped out the door and collected Mayla.

"Well, you're all in one piece, and that's more than I expect-ed," she said bluntly.

"More than I expected also. Lady Ackerley was very . . . condescending."

She gave a soft laugh. "You'll do, Miss Jessa, you'll do."

The tension of my conversation with Lady Ackerley faded before her approval, and though we exchanged a few simple remarks, the steady commentary Mayla had kept in town faded to a pleasant silence as we wandered the garden, allowing me a chance to collect my thoughts.

As we walked the crushed-stone paths, I noted they formed a pattern, an elaborate weaving of ways that resembled the trunk and branches of a great rowan tree. Along the path, hellebores in a variety of shades mingled beneath stately beech trees, and drooping laburnum sheltered snowdrops and sweet box. I luxuri-ated in the richness of color and texture that stretched on and on. When I came down the bottom of the stylized rowan path, I entered a beech-lined clearing with a bench in the center. I brushed my fingers across their soft new leaves, and their whis-pers wove a melody, alternately alluring and battering at my defenses.

Hear nothing.

I was here to seek answers, not succumb to the lures cast by bud and blossom. Resolutely, I turned my attention to exam-ining the terrain in an attempt to gain further insight on the Ackerley family from their estate, but even my best efforts could not fully drown out the alluring whispers. I clutched my reticule tighter and pressed on.

Throughout the extensive gardens, Lord Ackerley had installed additional gas lamps, the placement and fueling of which surely cost him a great deal. He'd even erected a series of fountains with mechanized automatons that moved about in tableaux on the waters. Every ostentatious adornment I encountered bespoke wealth—or at least a desire to convey power and resource to others. From what I could deduce of his character, either possible reason for wishing to oust Melle would make sense.

But it was far from conclusive evidence.

Once beyond the clearing, we found ourselves in another formal garden, which led down to the river. A wrought iron fence bordered its banks, enclosing the garden and the house. The stark black lines provided an unwelcome reminder of the rusalka, sprites, and various Otherworldly creatures who dwelt in rivers and waterways. Would these palings of iron, long held to repel denizens of the Otherworld, be sufficient to bar intrusion if hostile fae wished to access the estate? And what of the mill? The same river flowed through them both. Had it ever been plagued by fae?

I inquired of Mayla, and she shrugged. "Otherkind appear here more often than elsewhere, I'll grant, but we take precautions. It's most often those who wander astray that find themselves snared, not well-protected estates like this one."

We forged into a large shrubbery, so sheltered that one could no longer view the manor house. As the trees and bushes closed in around us, so did the whispers press upon me, creating a nagging ache at my temples that I did my best to ignore.

I quickened my pace, only to stumble over a root. I caught myself against the bole of a linden tree, and the world around me dimmed, then flared with a golden light. Through the shimmer, a figure appeared . . .

Isuel.

She stood among the trees, trepidation written across her face. She paced back and forth in front of the linden, peering occasionally down the path.

And then a tall, thick-set man strode into the shrubbery, his head lifted at an imperious angle, his attire of the latest mode. "I see you received my message."

"I did, my lord. You wished to speak about the mill?"

"Yes." He surveyed her head to toe. "It's of the utmost importance to me to have good relations within my town."

As he spoke, he reached out and caressed her cheek.

She stumbled back. "I beg your pardon, my lord, but that's not proper."

"Come, Isuel." He used her familiar name, though clearly there was no great acquaintance between them. "We're both adults. You're no innocent, but a woman who's been wed and borne children. No need to play coy."

"I'm not playing at anything." Isuel stumbled back. "I . . . I'd best go."

He snared her arm, pinning her in place. "We're not through yet."

Isuel struggled in vain, and an unpleasant smile twisted Lord Ackerley's features. But before he could touch her again, a young gardener appeared, rolling a barrow, his distinctive red hair gleaming even beneath the shadows of the trees.

Lord Ackerley abruptly released Isuel, and she fled like a rabbit freed from a snare.

"You blithering fool." Lord Ackerley wheeled upon the unfortunate gardener—

And someone tugged my arm, once, twice.

"Miss Jessa? Miss Jessa! Are you well?"

I wrenched away from the tree, my stomach churning. The world whirled about me as though I were a child once more, twirling in endless circles until balance was but a distant memory. I clutched at Mayla, and bit by bit, the greens and browns resolved themselves into familiar trees and shrubs.

What had befallen me?

Mayla supported me, her brown eyes wide. "Have you taken ill?"

I shook my head, pressing my lips together tightly. I dared not speak lest I cast up my accounts on Mayla.

"You'd better sit a moment." She took my arm and ushered me to a bench tucked deep within the shrubbery.

The warm wicker bench anchored me to the earth, and slowly the world balanced itself once more. Mayla waited, her features taut with concern. I needed to offer some explanation, but what? I fumbled for a reason that was both the truth and feeble excuse all tangled into one. "Forgive me. I . . . I should have kept a slower pace. I can't quite catch my breath, and I feel a bit faint."

I hoped she'd press no further, since it wasn't uncommon for ladies to come all over faint for one reason or another. In this at least, societal expectations worked in my favor.

"You do look pale. Perhaps you'd like me to drive back?"

"Yes, please. If we could just wait a moment . . ."

"Certainly. Take the time you require to recover." She gave me a sharp glance. "When you didn't answer, I feared for a moment you'd been caught in a fae-working or some such."

"Nothing so thrilling, I assure you." But could I offer such assurance? The bitter taste of fear filled my mouth. Mayla had broken me free of whatever unnatural influence gripped me, but what if I'd wandered the gardens alone? What fate would have befallen me?

I tucked my shaking hands into the folds of my gown, longing for Jade and the calm and comfort she brought. In her absence, I attended to my recitations, forcing my breath to even with each line. Once I could manage to stand, I followed Mayla back to the carriage.

Was this what led to madness in the fae-touched, the constant impingement of Other overriding one's own senses? Might one reach the point where it could be blocked no longer, and it overwhelmed body and soul? I clutched my skirts tighter. No matter, for once I left Milburn, surely I'd be free . . .

But what of those trapped here with a predator like Lord Ackerley? I cast a glance back at the shrubbery. Could I assume my peculiar experience represented truth? Or was it a glamour cast by some sort of hidden Otherkind for its entertainment? Or perhaps some unnatural influence of the nearby Crossing? Somehow I must determine the veracity of what I'd witnessed, if not the source as well. I climbed into the curricle, still slightly unsteady.

Mayla took the reins in capable hands and drove us off at a brisk trot. She shot me a single sideways glance, but otherwise remained quiet.

I composed myself enough to offer an apology. "Forgive me for cutting our visit short. I—"

"No need for excuses. Your reasons are your own, and I won't pry. I may speak my mind, but I don't press in where I'm not wanted." She flicked the reins, and the horses picked up pace.

"I—thank you." If I sought to dissemble, I'd only confirm there was more to my situation than I'd claimed. And after her kindness, I did not wish to deceive. Had I hurt her already with my reluctance to confide? I studied the curricle floor, the faint tracings of dust left by our footsteps and dozens of other passengers before imprinted across the dark surface. I dared not speak of what I did not understand, but I must try to inject some lightness into our conversation, while also pursuing the truth. "The gardens were truly remarkable. How many gardeners does Lord Ackerley employ to maintain such lovely grounds?"

"Oh, a good dozen at least." She rattled on a bit about the various gardeners and assistants and then said, "The older gardeners are quite loyal to him, but he has had trouble keeping newer staff members. He recently dismissed his latest assistant."

"Why?"

"According to Lord Ackerley, the lad was too lazy, though I must say I've observed no signs of it. He's applied himself to seeking work about town with a great deal of energy. He even came by the haberdashery to see if we wanted someone to run errands." Mayla clucked to the horses. "I believe he's working at the inn right now—at least, until Lord Ackerley gets word he's still in Milburn."

"You think he'll be forced to leave?"

She hesitated a moment. "I believe Lord Ackerley will exert his influence to make Milburn an unpleasant place for him, until he chooses to leave. It wouldn't be the first time."

I gripped my reticule tightly. "You say the assistant is rather young?"

Mayla nodded.

"Perhaps I've seen him." Not at the inn, but in my distressing encounter. "Does he have red hair and a lean face? With a sharpish sort of nose?"

"That's the fellow."

I sank back into the leather seat. Though I couldn't fathom the exact source, it seemed I'd witnessed the truth of the situation between Lord Ackerley and Isuel. Would his former gardener be willing to speak with me about Lord Ackerley? If the lad testified to the stratesman about what he'd seen, perhaps that would be sufficient cause to examine the mill's sabotage from a different angle.

My thoughts pressed upon me, making conversation difficult, but I forced myself to inquire about Mayla's business with the housekeeper, so my interest in the gardeners would hopefully avoid attracting notice.

Her lips tightened. "It was as I expected."

Then she fell into a welcome silence, and I stared at the horizon, unseeing. Lord and Lady Ackerley sought to dictate social mores for Milburn, and yet Lord Ackerley preyed upon whomever he desired. Did Lady Ackerley know? Even if she did, she was likely powerless to stop him, and so he acted unchecked.

After his altercation with Isuel, Lord Ackerley had every reason to sabotage the mill. This went beyond general resentment of her and Melle for upending what he believed to be the proper order and into far more personal territory of thwarted desire and wounded pride. He seemed the sort to make Isuel pay for spurning his unwelcome attentions, and what better way then by leaving her and her family destitute . . . and the path open to install a miller of his choosing or even build a mill of his own?

All I'd uncovered today pointed to Lord Ackerley being the responsible party in the sabotage, but such a man, holding wealth, power, and influence in Milburn, would be near impossible to stop—especially since my only evidence was an illusory experience. To turn the attention of the stratesman toward him would require more concrete information. Even were the former gardener willing to testify, what he witnessed might prove insufficient to engage the authorities.

After all, with a few well-placed words, Lord Ackerley could sabotage the career of a stratesman as easily as he could damage the mill. I must gather any facts I could and hope they would permit his condemnation, if he were as guilty as he appeared.

I passed a restless night, my dreams broken by all manner of disturbing images: magnificent, malevolent rusalka tempting Lady Ackerley past the iron palings and into the river; Lord Ackerley looming over Isuel; the Dyott sinkhole growing to swallow the cottage and mill alike; and black-clad Vigilists pounding down our door to haul Nelda away.

At last, I woke with a gasp. A bird chirruped outside the window, and the great oak rose stolid and stately beyond the glass, unshaken by imagined terrors. Nelda had already left the bedchamber, and the murmur of her conversation with Aunt Caris drifted into the room. Since their excursion together, Aunt Caris had inclined further in her favor. Evidently, Nelda had remained quiet and troubled during their day of travel but comported herself with all propriety, sealing her in Aunt Caris's mind as an unfortunate in need of aid.

In response to her kindness, Nelda had grown more comfortable as well, which removed one burden.

I dressed hurriedly. If Aunt Caris didn't require my assistance, I'd seek to learn more from the townsfolk this morning, starting with the former gardener. A visit to the bakery to see if I could discover what Lord Ackerley had said to influence the baker might also prove illuminating.

At the dining table, I gratefully accepted the steaming cup of tea that Aunt Caris offered, in hopes it would lift the fog from my thoughts. But no sooner had I taken a sip than a sharp rap sounded at the door.

Nelda flinched. "May I go?"

Aunt Caris folded her hands. "I think that would be best. I can't imagine who would call this early, but you should wait in the sitting room until we find out who's here. No sense reminding them of your presence."

After Nelda vanished, I opened the door. The stratesman

waited on the other side, the white insignia on his shoulder a stark contrast to the otherwise earthen tones of his garments. The lines furrowing his forehead suggested advanced years, as did a beard the curling texture of forester moss, liberally sprinkled with gray. Still, he held himself tall and erect, altogether an imposing figure. My stomach twisted.

Had he come for Nelda after all?

"I'm Stratesman Bancroft. Forgive the disruption, but I'd like to speak with you." While polite, his firm tone permitted no denial.

"With me?"

"And your aunt."

He glanced past me, and I clung to the door as if it were a lifeline. I wanted to shut it in his face, but that would cause far greater trouble. So I stepped back. "Please come in."

Aunt Caris forced a stiff smile. "How can we help you, Stratesman Bancroft?"

"It's about the young woman, Nelda." He straightened his cuffs. "I'm not certain you're aware, but you're housing the foremost suspect in the disturbing events at Dyott Mill."

Aunt Caris shot me a glance which contained more than a hint of fear. Now that she'd concerned herself with Nelda, if the girl were taken away, it would cause Aunt Caris further distress.

I shrank inward and wrapped my arms around my chest. "We've heard the rumors."

"I'll get straight to the point," Stratesman Bancroft said. "There's been more trouble at the mill."

Aunt Caris paled. "Surely not."

"It happened last night. I've just come from there."

"What happened?" I asked.

"Yesterday, Mrs. Hopkins received the items she needed to

carry out repairs on the mill. They were all stolen sometime after dark."

Aunt Caris leaned forward, her gown rustling. "But no injury?"

"No, Miss Caldwell."

"Thank the Infinite." But her features still bore an unusual pallor.

"Nelda could have easily carried out the theft. As the former miller's daughter, she would have known how to access the mill and where supplies were kept."

"There must be others with that knowledge as well." If only I'd had more time before the stratesman arrived, I might have presented him with a factual case against Lord Ackerley. But if I brought up my theory now, with nothing but my unsettling encounter to back it, he'd most likely dismiss it without a second thought—and be disinclined to listen in the future, when I had actual evidence to present.

"Perhaps." Stratesman Bancroft lifted a shoulder. "But there's only so long I can look past the obvious culprit for a more far-fetched explanation."

"Nelda was here last night, so she couldn't have stolen anything," I said. Jade twined around my ankles, the fur on her ruff rising at the tension in my voice. "She slept on the trundle in my bedchamber."

"She might have left at any time. You didn't lock her in."

"That's true, but I didn't sleep well. Surely I would have heard if she departed."

"Maybe." He stared down his hawklike nose, as if he was examining me for any hint of deception. "But can you swear she was there all night? No shadow of doubt?"

I caught my lip between my teeth. At some point in the night, I'd looked over at the trundle and discovered Nelda absent. I'd assumed she'd gone to use the facilities. It hadn't been long—or so I thought. But how did one measure the passing hours when drifting from disturbed dreams to uneasy waking? If I was wrong, if I swore beyond the bounds of my knowledge . . . I knotted my hands. "I am reasonably certain. To travel to the mill and back and to take the supplies . . . that would have required most of the night."

"But would you swear before the Magister?" He shot the question almost before I finished speaking.

"No," I whispered. "I cannot swear."

He leaned back, satisfied at last. "I'll need to see Nelda."

I checked the protest that rose to my lips. I couldn't deny him, for I had no authority here. But if I found him daunting, then he must terrify Nelda. I glanced toward the closed door. "May I stay with her? She's experienced enough upset."

"Your sympathy does you credit. But she may be a danger." He stroked his graying beard. "Even if I'd not come to question her, I'd have come to warn you—best to distance yourself. If she's truly responsible, I can't predict how she'll act next."

Aunt Caris stirred a spoonful of sugar into her tea, with rather more of a clatter than usual. "If you're certain Nelda committed the crimes, then why do you allow her continued liberty?"

"She has a motive. But the evidence is less clear." Stratesman Bancroft frowned. "And I don't want to waste the Magister's time."

His measured words suggested he kept far more hidden than he'd revealed. What else did he know? I swallowed a rising sense of alarm. If I didn't uncover clear evidence against Lord Ackerley soon, it might be too late for Nelda. I shifted to place myself between the stratesman and the room where Nelda hid. "I see.

I'd still like to be there when you speak with her, if you'll permit."

"If you're that determined, I'll allow it this time. Perhaps when you see how she acts, you'll trust the authorities to handle matters properly." Again he tugged at his cuffs. "Regardless, I suggest you stop housing her at once. I'm not sure how you persuaded Mr. Wilkins to let her stay."

I wasn't either, unless the Otherness I sensed in Milburn was somehow involved, but no sense confessing it. Instead, I crossed to the adjoining door. "I'll fetch Nelda."

But when I entered the sitting room, the window stood open, curtains fluttering in the spring breeze.

Nelda was gone.

CHAPTER 8

Oh, the upset Nelda left in her wake. Stratesman Bancroft appeared to take her flight as confirmation of guilt and determined to hunt her down at once. Aunt Caris wavered between concern for Nelda and fear that perhaps she was responsible for the events at the mill after all. And I . . . I worried.

If I *was* entirely mistaken about Lord Ackerley and Nelda was guilty, then her freedom meant danger for Melle and the mill. But if I was correct and Nelda was innocent, then her flight increased her own danger. If she'd been listening at the door, she would have known about the theft and heard her name blackened further. Her choice to run spoke to me of desperation rather than guilt. And who wouldn't feel desperate? If the stratesman took Nelda and she wasn't the culprit, she would suffer the rest of her life for a crime she had never committed.

Certainly, I didn't expect Lord Ackerley to confess in her defense. If he thought nothing of forcing his attentions on unwilling victims, then why would he spare a moment of regret for an innocent woman taking the blame for his crime? If he was the responsible party, he might even congratulate himself for pinning the sabotage on Nelda.

After Stratesman Bancroft departed, Aunt Caris changed her plans for the day, announcing her intent to persuade Melle and her family to take haven at the inn temporarily while the stratesman attempted to sort the matter. Given Melle's determined personality, I struggled to imagine her abandoning her property and livestock to someone intent on sabotage. But I hoped I was wrong.

Since I'd no intention of letting Aunt Caris face Melle by herself, I postponed my plans to seek out the red-haired gardener. The visit from Stratesman Bancroft had already shaken Aunt Caris. What would another encounter with Melle do? Time had only given Melle greater cause to be angry—and Aunt Caris was a safe target for her wrath. No, I could just as easily scour the mill grounds for evidence first and then speak with the lad when we returned to the inn.

Aunt Caris bustled back into the room. "Are you ready?"

I fetched my hat and shawl from the stand beside the door. "I am now."

Jade protested at once with a bone-chilling yowl, and this time, all my efforts to coax her to remain failed. So I lifted her into my arms, and we were on our way, Jade giving a purr of satisfaction as we walked down to the courtyard.

After we'd rattled along a bit, Aunt Caris turned to me, face drawn. "I'll need to talk with Melle alone."

"Aunt Caris, I don't think—"

"This is my concern, dear. Not yours." She tugged her shawl more closely around her shoulders. "I only agreed to your coming so you wouldn't be alone at the inn if Stratesman Bancroft decided to return with more questions. He seemed a great deal upset by Nelda's disappearance."

If only Aunt Caris were amenable to my assistance, matters would be much simpler. I traced the seam of my glove with one finger, seeking the right approach. "Perhaps if we could help Melle figure out who is sabotaging the mill, she wouldn't need to relocate and—"

"Heavens, no. I know you enjoy puzzles, but don't let your curiosity lead you astray, dear. This isn't like those dreadful mystery tales you enjoy. It's a dangerous situation best left to the stratesmen to manage." She lifted a leather satchel and passed it to me. "You haven't had much opportunity to sketch since we arrived, so I brought your materials for you. I thought perhaps you'd enjoy capturing some of the scenes around the mill. Despite everything that's happened, it's quite lovely."

Her tone brooked no argument. She still saw Ada, Ainslie, and me as children to shelter, never considering we might want to help her as she'd helped us over the years. But there was more than one way to offer aid.

Before he'd left, the stratesman had indicated he would arrest Nelda in absence of another suspect. Never mind the risks, I would do whatever was necessary to uncover the truth, freeing Melle and her family from the increasingly dangerous situation at the mill and Aunt Caris from her entanglement in the whole affair. If Aunt Caris expected me to sketch, then roaming about the property and examining the scenery would raise no questions.

Our coachman drew up a safe distance away from the cottage, and Ives helped Aunt Caris down. I climbed out by myself, and Jade gingerly picked her way along beside me, a sure sign her healing had progressed well, despite my inexperience in treatment.

The waters of the sinkhole lurked black and ominous before us, absorbing the light cast by the sun. I averted my eyes to a happier sight: the children playing in the barnyard where Isuel fed the chickens.

She waved a hand in welcome, but as we drew closer, the strain etched on her features became clear. "Good morning."

Aunt Caris offered a greeting in return, one which distinctly lacked her usual cheer. "I've come to speak with Melle, and I hoped Jessa might do some sketching, if you'll grant permission."

My face warmed. Only a senseless and carefree miss would yearn to further her own artistic endeavors while danger beset those around her. And yet, this portrayal suited my ultimate purpose, so I choked down a protest and awaited an answer.

"Certainly she may, though things are rather in disarray."

Sketch pad in hand and pencils tucked into my reticule, I strolled from the barnyard, collecting Jade as I went. She'd strayed perilously close to the sinkhole, sniffing at some peculiar cuplike plants. I'd no desire to draw near enough to examine them more closely, and when I called to her, she bounded to my side. Together, we walked toward the mill.

If Lord Ackerley had sent men to steal the supplies and they'd left any sign of their passing, I had the greatest chance of finding traces near the mill or along the river path, where they were less likely to be seen.

The footpath wended from the barnyard to the mill and beyond, skirting the edge of the river. Footsteps marked every part of the path, along with signs of a single wheel, perhaps from a barrow. The mill itself rose above the wide river, its moss-stained stones and steep rooflines enchanting even with its tremendous wheel stilled.

A sigh escaped me. Who was I to think I could uncover evidence a stratesman had failed to find?

Yet I must try. I studied the soft ground between the river

and the mill closely. Water had recently saturated the earth leading to the main door of the mill, as though the river had risen beyond its banks—peculiar, since we'd had no recent rainfall—and unlike the footpath, this stretch of ground bore scarcely any signs of human passage. The only marks were a single set of prints left by boots like those the stratesman wore—perhaps a remnant of his investigation.

If Lord Ackerley had sent men, the process of removing the equipment should have left traces. How could anyone have passed over the sodden earth without leaving a mark?

Jade leapt over the muck and stretched herself out on the wide, flat stone in front of the door. Near where her tail twitched, a glint of silver caught my eye. I stepped closer and found small, shimmering cuplike plants clustered at the edge of the stone, resembling those I'd seen from a distance near the sinkhole. At once, their presence impressed itself against me, vibrant, living, *Other*. An unfamiliar scent wafted around me, fresh and sparkling like the world after a storm.

Not again, not now. I closed my eyes and drew a deep breath, then turned my back on the unusual blossoms. The movement proved insufficient, so I rehearsed my favorite passage of the Script, one memorized during countless Sundays attending Liturgy with my family. I murmured it backward and forward, until the pulsing awareness began to fade.

Jade returned to my side and nuzzled my ankle just above my boot, the sensation grounding me. If I wished to uncover the truth, I couldn't afford to grow distracted by the sensations that plagued me.

I lifted her once more and walked around the corner, back toward the footpath. This side of the watermill faced the cottage and did offer another possible entry point. But where the main entrance boasted double doors of dark walnut, wide enough to allow large loads into the mill, this was a small single door, perhaps meant to add convenience for the miller. Although the jumble of prints on the footpath might well conceal any number of individuals accessing this entrance, I couldn't imagine any man or woman of sense choosing this approach. Not only would the small door make it difficult to remove materials quickly, the thieves would be far more exposed.

I surveyed the scene once more. Could Lord Ackerley have sent men to access the mill by water, in order to leave less evidence of their passing? Without a boat, it would be difficult to test that theory, but perhaps I could borrow one and return. Regardless, they still would have had to pass over the land immediately surrounding the mill. Which brought me back to where I'd started.

Something didn't add up, but since both doors were locked, I could examine nothing else here. If I pressed on, perhaps I'd find a trace of human passing elsewhere. I continued up the path toward the weir, drawn by the sound of water rushing over its crest. Stately willows lined this section of the river, their boughs lowering to sweep the banks.

As I watched their graceful dance, the knot of tension inside eased—until I wove between two particularly tall willows. When their branches brushed over me, I felt as though a thousand insects writhed across my skin. Once more, Milburn and my heightened emotions had worked against me, lowering my defenses. I rubbed my hands along my arms, trying to shake the alarming sensation, but it refused to relent.

And then I looked up. A webbed nest of devorworms stretched between low-hanging limbs. Once they hatched, they would consume the tree and then wreak havoc on the rest of the mill property as they grew, a source of mindless—and ceaseless —destruction. They were uncommon, a pestilence that had been mostly eradicated. The back of my neck prickled. Had someone placed them here, in another attempt at sabotage?

At least I could do something about this problem. "Don't worry, I'll see you fixed in no time."

I stood on tiptoes to detach the sticky mass from the tree. It sagged ominously, the weight of the eggs within threatening to burst the confines of the webbing. I shuddered and hurled it into the river. Threads of silk clung to my fingers, and I scrubbed my hands on my skirt to remove them.

With the devorworm nest gone, the writhing sensation eased at once, and the boughs of the willow relaxed. Jade sniffed at my palms, as if to assure herself no trace remained, then tapped her nose against me in approval.

A silvery glint in the waters caught my eye, and I drew nearer, Jade trailing after me. Below the weir, the water swirled in a pattern counter to the flow of the river.

Peculiar.

There was no sign of the cause, and after a few moments, I almost turned away. But the leaves of the willow rustled, the branches sweeping toward the waters, a repetitive motion that urged me to stay. I waited a minute longer, and the churning of the river intensified. Amid the silvery ripples, sinuous forms revealed themselves—as though the water took on human shape, lithe and gleaming in the sunlight.

Water sprites.

I staggered back.

Jade growled deep in her chest.

And my breath caught at their beauty. The allure of their forms and features caused me to reach for my sketchbook without thought, as if I could ever capture their exotic faces on the page. But even as my fingers closed around the leather book, I hesitated. Did I want to capture such unnatural beauty?

However striking, their features lacked any nuance of human emotion or sympathy, as though they were crafted by some master hand with perfect form but no feeling. The storm-fresh scent I'd first caught by the doorstone filled the air, along with a burgeoning sense of menace.

What I should do was flee, run from the danger they presented . . . but then I'd never gain answers.

A female sprite with dark-green hair resembling water thyme surged upward. *We'll soon be free.*

Free! Other voices echoed in exultation. Their skin shimmered pale silvery-blue, and the little clothing they wore was white as the foam where the water churned over the mill, a diaphanous, clinging material that scarcely concealed their powerful, sculpted frames.

They seem unconcerned with my presence, as if they expected to remain unseen and unheard. And so they should. Everyone knew water sprites only shed their concealing glamour when they found prey they wished to lure into the depths. And even then, it was said they used a wordless, compelling song that enthralled mortals, drawing them to their deaths. Since they were low fae, their language was beyond human understanding.

I shouldn't be able to perceive them, much less hear distinctive words . . . unless Father's well-argued explanation for my affliction was incorrect. Could I . . . did I bear the taint of fae-touch?

My heart thumped an uneven rhythm; my body went cold. I almost closed my eyes and clenched my fists over my ears—anything to banish the fae from my awareness, to pretend a moment longer that I bore no such taint.

But no.

Whatever else I may be, whatever fate lay in store for me

after this, I refused to be a coward. I forced myself to look and *listen*.

Another sprite surfaced closer to the weir, his pale-blue hair cropped close and his eyes dark as the river during a storm. *A paltry theft. My plan was better. May be entertaining to watch them scramble. But may not be enough.*

Not so paltry for mortals. Their resources are few.

Small plans best. A third sprite leapt and splashed in the depths. *Best not draw attention from the Courts.*

What have they to say to it? It's our right to claim bargain.

I lost my grip on my sketchbook, and it clattered to the ground, while I remained rooted in place. Once again, the urge to blot them out swept over me, as I'd done so many times before when something peculiar edged its way onto my mental canvas.

Instead, I stood still. Open. Waiting.

Yes, yes. A female sprite clapped her hands. *They must hold to the sworn word.*

Foolish mortals. To think bindings can be broken. The blue-haired male swept his arms in an arc through the river, and I caught a glimpse of pale webbing between his fingers. *They shall pay.*

Yes! Fierce glee shone on the face of the nearest female sprite. *Girl removed devorworms. We could bring more?*

A sprite taller than the rest lifted his head and broad shoulders above the waters, which swirled around his muscular form as if he'd been a boulder. *No. Our play with mortals was pleasant. But I tire.* His eyes glinted like sun-kissed water. *Time for river to be freed of bonds, time bargain is upheld.*

There was an echo of agreement, then with a swirl, they vanished below the surface of the water. The ripples soon faded, and the river became placid again. I sank to the ground beneath the willow, wrapping my arms around my legs.

After a final hiss at the river, Jade strolled over and nudged my hand, which trembled as I attempted a reassuring pat.

What I'd seen today meant my experiences were not some aberration brought on by emotional strain, as Father had claimed and I'd accepted, but a reality I shouldn't perceive—unless I was bent by some inward flaw, some taint of the Otherworld. The distress and shame it would bring to my family . . . they might never recover, and the knowledge sat like a block of ice within my chest.

Unbidden, a memory I'd long tried to bury emerged. One beautiful autumn day at Caldwell House, I'd played in the gardens alone, as was my wont, content in a world of peace and beauty . . . until old Mrs. Murton had bolted out from behind the rose hedge.

She'd charged forward and gripped my arm, her frizzled hair wisping wildly round her head like tangle moss in spring. "You see them, child? You see? I know you do, you must. They're everywhere."

Her eyes, wide and staring, darted frantically from side to side. I struggled to free myself from her grip, but her long, unkempt nails dug into my skin, holding me captive.

"They'll imprison us all." She moaned, long and low. "What's to be done, what's to be done?"

Then she staggered back, eyes growing even wider. "I should have known." She wielded her ward-pendant against me like a weapon. "Keep back."

I stumbled away, tripping over a root, skinning my elbow.

And then, blessedly, the gardener appeared, along with Father—not distant and detached as he'd become after Mother's death, but fully present, vibrant and strong. "What's all this?"

Mrs. Murton spun around, her ward-pendant still uplifted. "Watch yourself. We're in danger, every one of us."

The gardener paled. "It's the fae-touch. It's taken her. I told her not to go digging round the dells, nor take them rook-foot toadstools. But she wouldn't listen."

"I fear you're correct." Grim lines furrowed Father's face. "I'd hoped to avoid it, but she's too far gone. We'd best call in the Vigil. See to it, Thompkins. I'll stay here with her."

Mrs. Murton paid Father no heed, her attention fixed on something I could not perceive. "Quiet, quiet! Oh, won't someone make them *stop*."

Then she clapped both hands over her ears and sank to the ground.

And I'd fled the gardens, seeking Mother, yet I did not find the refuge I expected with her. After offering me brief reassurance, she went to Father and protested the involvement of the Vigil.

In this rare instance, Father had stood firm. "I won't have her endangering our family or our tenants. She must go."

After that day, I never saw Mrs. Murton again. When I asked Mother later why the fae would influence mortal minds in such a way, she became remote, almost detached. "Such matters are not for children to consider, Jessa."

It stung, for Mother spoke freely with us about all things. Fae-touch must be more dreadful than I'd ever dreamed, if Mother refused to speak of it . . .

I shook free of the memory. What would Mother say if she still lived, if she knew I might carry such a taint? Worse still, would I become like Mrs. Murton if I could not swiftly regain control? Would Father himself summon the Vigil, this time for me? I reached for Jade and held her close, her warmth slowly seeping through my skin.

Perhaps . . . perhaps there was still another explanation for this. Perhaps Father was not wrong. Perhaps what I'd experienced today had nothing to do with fae-touch. None of my experiences prior to our arrival here had included fae, so maybe the encounter with the sprites, along with the other oddities I'd endured in Milburn, came simply from my proximity to the Crossing and the fae encounters common in edgetowns, rather than fae-touch exerting its claim.

Oh please, let it be true.

Jade wiggled, and I loosened my grasp. Regardless, I couldn't think about it now, couldn't consider what all of this meant for the future, for my family. Not when the fate of Melle and her family, of Aunt Caris and Nelda, hung in the balance. As I'd long practiced, I stuffed the errant thoughts and feelings into the cage of thorns within.

Then I rested my back against the hoary bark of the willow, and it pulsed with vitality and vigor. My mind cleared slightly.

But clarity brought no comfort. I'd been dreadfully wrong. There'd been no trace of human passage at the mill doors, only sodden ground and Otherworldly growth, because no mortal bore responsibility for this crime.

Like Stratesman Bancroft had with Nelda, I'd leapt to the assumption that motive for a crime meant guilt. I'd so feared the sensations of Other that I refused to consider the evidence that might have pointed to an Otherwordly culprit: the defenses the wealthy Ackerleys had in place along the river to protect their property—lacking here at the mill—the unusual plants growing at the sinkhole and by the mill, the unnatural sinkhole itself, and the eerie laugh I'd heard.

I pulled my knees to my chest. Lord Ackerley may have attempted assault against Isuel, may have resented the presence of Melle and her family in his town, may have every motive in the world to wish them to suffer, may be a deplorable man in every sense of the word—but he'd not committed the theft, nor the sabotage against them. And the true culprits were far more dangerous.

Since I *had* perceived the sprites, whatever the reason, a responsibility fell on my shoulders, impossible to deny or ignore. If Lord Ackerley had been the saboteur, it would have been difficult to prove his guilt, but in time, I might have found enough evidence to convince the stratesman to take a look at him.

But this? To explain it meant great risk, assuming Stratesman Bancroft even believed me. And if he did, he would surely summon the Vigil, given all such activities fell under their province.

The ice returned to lodge in my chest. If the Vigil were involved, I could only foresee disaster. If past practice held true, they would likely seize the mill and surrounding area—claiming it necessary to protect the mortals in the region—and banish Melle and her family to fend for themselves.

And I couldn't pretend, even to myself, I didn't have personal fears.

If I brought the Vigilists here, if I confessed how I'd witnessed the sprites, they'd take me to an Institution, and I'd lose my freedom and my family forever.

No, somehow I had to extricate the mill from the clutches of the water sprites—and clear Nelda in the process—without involving the Vigil.

Steps heavy, I padded back to the house, Jade sticking closer than my shadow, her presence a comfort. If I was to manage the situation on my own, I needed more information, both about the sprites and whatever bargain they had formed. The facts as I knew them suggested it preceded Melle's arrival. After years of running the mill peacefully, Nelda's father had died—and somehow, in the short interval after his passing, the mill had sustained sufficient damage to cause it to go for a lower price, which had then made it affordable to Melle. And Melle in turn had suffered one trouble after another, unaware of the true source.

Or was she?

Somehow, I must find out. I followed the path to the back door of the cottage. It sat open, letting fresh spring air into the kitchen, and I slipped through.

Isuel bent over some dough, kneading and shaping loaves. She gave a worn smile as I entered. "Did you discover any fitting scenes to sketch?"

"There are certainly some lovely views." I demurred, avoiding the horrifying truth. "How did Nelda's father die?"

It was a graceless comment, with no natural transition, and Isuel looked at me oddly. "He drowned, or so we were told."

Drowned. I collapsed into a chair. I had little doubt the song of the sprites had lured him to his end. They would have toyed with him until his weary limbs maintained their buoyancy no longer . . . and he sank to the depths. If they'd killed him, what did that mean about the bargain? Had he made it? Had he violated it?

And more importantly, did Melle violate it by living here? Could her family safely remain? The chill spread down my spine, and Jade leapt onto my lap, calming me. I couldn't rightfully make that decision on their behalf, not if they had no notion of what was happening here. But how could I broach the matter without giving Melle yet another secret to hold over Aunt Caris?

No time remained to decide, for Melle and Aunt Caris appeared in the doorway. Isuel looked from the strained expression on Aunt Caris's face to the set stance of her mother and then ventured, "Miss Caldwell, I've been told that you have much experience with needlework. I've run into a bit of a problem with a dress I'm making for Essie. Would you come look?"

"Of course." Aunt Caris followed Isuel from the room.

I blessed Isuel's peacemaking tendencies and the opportunity they opened. Before Melle attempted to depart, I took a deep breath and plunged in. "If . . . if you suspected fae were responsible for the attacks here, would you want the Vigil to be involved?"

To my surprise, she paled. "You've been listening to Aebbe." She leaned in. "I know she presents a convincing argument that the fae are behind everything, but she doesn't know what she's saying, not truly. In some ways she's sharp as ever, but in others, age and loss—they've addled her wits."

"But if she was right . . ." I fumbled for words.

"Right or wrong, it doesn't matter." Melle drew herself up, the familiar battle stance returning. "If you bring the Vigil here, they'll haul her away, take everything. More loss, after Eadric and Dale—it's unthinkable. You *must* leave them out of this."

Perhaps I yielded too quickly, because her command supported my own desires. But surely there was another way out, one that didn't cause greater distress and destruction. I had only time to murmur assent before Aunt Caris returned to the kitchen. She offered subdued farewells, and we took our leave, Jade prowling alongside.

Outside the cottage, the shadows of the trees stretched long across the lawn. We climbed into the carriage and departed, Aunt Caris maintaining a rigid silence.

Finally, I ventured to ask, "What did Melle say?"

"Foolish woman. She won't consider leaving the mill, no matter the danger. She insists we stick to the plan, though I've tried to explain . . ." She rubbed her temples. "I can't discuss it further, not now."

"Please don't worry, Aunt Caris. It will work out." I stared into the gloom of the forest, where pools of dark gathered beneath ancient trees. I must resolve this . . . but how?

CHAPTER 9

After Aunt Caris and I dined, I excused myself to write to Ada and Ainslie. We might have our differences, but oh, I longed for their presence. If Ada were here, she would listen with great sympathy as I expressed my fears, and Ainslie would invent some wild adventure to distract me from my woes. With the two of them at my side, I could face anything.

But even if they were here, I'd feel alone. For I couldn't confess the truth, not even to them.

My eyes stung, and the letters blurred on the page. I blinked them back into focus and, with effort, crafted an abridged account of our experiences in Milburn. I even included a small watercolor of the Ackerley gardens, though with no hint of my true purpose there. With each word, my determination grew. I would solve this, and Aunt Caris and I would return to Avons, fae and fancies put to rest.

Letter in hand, I ventured down to the welcoming room.

Mr. Wilkins stood behind the counter, jotting notes in a ledger. When I approached, he looked up.

"Good evening, Miss Jessa." His dark brows lowered. "I heard Nelda abandoned you, after all you did for her. Sorry you were taken in, but can't say I'm sad to see her go."

"No, I imagine not." I smiled to soften the words. "I'm off to post a letter, and I hoped you might tell me if Milburn has a lending library."

"We have a fine one. The Hollace family supplied a starting collection some years back, and then, of course, our subscribers keep it going."

"Wonderful. Are they open in the evening?"

"Not past dinner, Miss Jessa. Nor should you go out this late." He braced against the counter. "Dusk is an unchancy hour in these parts. If you leave your letter with me, I'll have one of the lads post it in the morning."

The quiet murmur of the fountain brought back an echo of the water over the weir and the sounds of the water sprites. I shuddered. I'd no desire to risk an encounter with any sort of fae, not with my reserves worn so low. "Thank you, that's very kind."

But I couldn't give up my quest for understanding. I handed over the letter, along with another question. "Do you have a loremaster in Milburn?"

Loremasters studied the Otherworld, and aside from the Vigil—who guarded their information like the crown jewels— they possessed the greatest store of knowledge about the Otherkind. Some claimed they were no more than tale-tellers who offered guesswork and supposition, while others said they held hard-won insights. As with anything concerning the fae, it was difficult to discern truth from falsehood, rumor, or legend. Despite my interest in learning from them, I'd always avoided loremasters, fearing they might perceive the aberration within me. But now, I had to set such fears aside, because speaking with a loremaster might offer insight on how to drive away the sprites.

"We have one of sorts—Leofric Heard." Mr. Wilkins tapped the end of his pen against the ledger. "But he's not like most loremasters. He doesn't aim to share his knowledge, and he's none too welcoming to visitors. He's grown rather abrasive in his old age, and I'd hate for a lady such as yourself to endure his ill temper."

"I see." Why couldn't Mr. Heard have been a storyteller who delighted in enthralling an audience? I rubbed my temples. "That doesn't sound pleasant."

Perhaps I could avoid the loremaster—and the attendant risks—altogether and find the answers I sought within the town library. Oh, how I hoped.

In the morning, Aunt Caris appeared more herself. She intended to write and post some letters, though I couldn't imagine who else remained to beseech for funds, and she offered her blessing to my plans to visit the lending library. Most libraries didn't welcome pets, so I'd had no choice but to leave Jade behind once more, despite her pronounced displeasure.

A gentle breeze tugged my skirts as I strolled down the cobbled street, and the heads of the dayharts planted along the market square bobbed as I passed, their song golden and triumphant in the early light.

I closed my eyes and drew a deep breath, forcing myself to recite a familiar passage of Script to distract my attention. It only partially drowned out the song. I quickened my pace, seeking the tall, narrow building that housed the library. It sat at the far corner of the square, its cheery yellow door an invitation to visitors. Inside, I received a generous welcome from an older woman with eyes the warm brown of gold-elm leaves in autumn. She introduced herself as Miss Hollace, and after I explained my purpose in the most general terms, she graciously permitted me to review their reference materials without a subscription.

I forced myself to ignore the trove of intriguing books within, instead attending to the most promising tomes. In *Pemberton's Encyclopedia of Otherkind*, I flipped past the substantial section on Otherworldly beasts—dragons, griffins, and the like—and onto the low fae, entities like brownies, nisi, and sylphs, until I found the entry I sought:

WATER SPRITES

Low fae. Dwell in clans known as shivers. Fiercely territorial. When glamoured, they remain invisible to the mortal eye, their movements resembling natural ripples and currents and their voices becoming as the whispers of the waters.

They only shed their glamour when they wish to lure mortal prey into the depths. Even then, they speak no distinguishable words; they only release a song that clouds the mind and ends in death. To avoid falling victim to their wiles, one must stuff the ears with molded beeswax when venturing through their territory, a precaution recommended to all travelers through Crossing territories.

It was sparse and offered no more than I recalled from my past readings, besides a reminder of their territorial nature, which was hardly a boon in this situation. I snapped the book shut.

An hour's work had revealed nothing else of note, leaving only the loremaster as a source of further information. No other choice remained, unless I wished to abandon the mill to the nonexistent mercy of the sprites. Ignoring the sinking sensation within, I followed the directions provided by Miss Hollace, though she too warned me Mr. Heard didn't take to visitors, and I'd likely be turned away.

Like the Ackerleys, Mr. Heard had fortified his house with iron at the entries. In addition, the gardens surrounding his cottage held a selection of plants believed to repel fae—red verbena, marsh marigold, and Saint John's wort. They murmured fiercely as I swept up the white stone walk, as though they wished to drive me away along with any encroaching fae. Their militant whispers assaulted my senses as I approached the bright red door, but I refused to flee—not with what Aunt Caris stood to suffer if I forsook my efforts.

I lifted the bronze knocker and rapped softly. I risked offense by coming unchaperoned to the home of a single man, but given his advanced years, I hoped it would cause no rumors. I didn't have to wait long to find out.

A young woman opened the door, and she turned out to be his niece, who tended his affairs daily. Her presence eliminated one worry but introduced another. The more people who heard the questions I asked, the greater chance stories would spread.

After we exchanged introductions, I said, "I hope it's not too much trouble, but I've never traveled so close to a Crossing before, and I'd dearly love to hear lore about the fae." All true, so far as it went. I forced myself to keep my tone light. "I've been told Mr. Heard has extensive knowledge."

"Indeed he does, but he's in no mood for visitors. I'm afraid you've made a wasted trip."

"Wait!" a man bellowed from the other room. "Ask her what she'd do if she found a lost horse near the river, saddled and bridled, but with no owner in sight?"

He was a loremaster, so the question must relate to Otherkind, not ethics, but in either case, the answer was simple. I pitched my voice louder than usual. "I would examine its hooves to see if it was a kelpie. If it was, I would distance myself. If it was not, I would seek its owner to restore it."

"You show some amount of sense, more than most addlepated young ladies can boast." He was still bellowing from the depths of the house. "But tell me this. How do you distinguish between a kelpie and njuggle?"

"They're close relatives, but the Other nature of the njuggle displays itself in the tail, which even their glamour cannot fully conceal, while the kelpie reveals itself in its hooves."

"Can either be tamed?"

I tapped a finger against my lips. It was fortunate he'd chosen this topic, because the idea of a fae horse had captivated me as a girl, and I'd read a copious number of legends on the subject. "While most who made such attempts lost their lives, if the tales are to believed, Anise of Hartley managed to tame a njuggle with a scripted bridle and silver bit. She earned its friendship and later offered it freedom."

"Hmph. The truth of that legend is dubious, but I suppose it's good enough to earn you a chance. Mind you come along quick." His stentorian tones echoed down the hallway. "I don't have time to waste."

His niece blushed. "Pardon him. He's used to having his way, and he has odd notions at times."

Odd I could manage. Some of the tension eased from my shoulders. "It's no trouble."

I followed her to a room that smelled of old leather and pipe smoke, lined with orderly bookshelves. The whitewashed walls bore pen-and-ink drawings of various Otherkind: dragons soaring over open fields, shellycoats swarming through a river, and all sorts of fae, high and low alike.

Beside the hearth, Mr. Heard sat ensconced in a well-stuffed chair, his grizzled head shrouded in a cloud of smoke rings. "Let me take a look at you."

It took everything in me not to shrink from his scrutiny. It wasn't lascivious; rather, he was assessing, seeking something, his brown eyes keen beneath wildly bushing brows. I didn't dare speak, lest I earn his rejection.

At last, he nodded. "Ask your questions."

I glanced at his niece, who looked between us with evident interest. Would she carry a full report to the village gossips?

He followed my gaze and waved his niece away. "You're not wanted."

She shook her head, but seemed undisturbed by his rudeness. Before she left, she told me, "I'll be preparing his luncheon if you need anything."

When the door shut behind her, he motioned to a nearby chair. "Sit here."

I sat.

"What is it you want?"

I shifted, and the straw-stuffed cushion beneath me crackled. "As I mentioned to your niece, I'm interested in learning the lore Milburn has about the fae—"

"Don't give me the namby-pamby nonsense you handed her. If you wanted stories, the villagers offer them in plenty. Why are you *here*?"

"I have questions that need reliable answers."

He leaned forward, his dark eyes like coals in his wrinkled face. "Why?"

"Because I need to understand the fae in order to protect those I love." The words wrenched painfully from me.

"Do you mean to confront them?"

My mouth went dry. How much did he know? It was clear he'd permit no dissembling, so I sat up straighter. "If I must."

"Then I'll tell you what I can." He puffed harder on his pipe. "Won't have your blood on my hands though, if your plans go awry."

"I don't expect you to bear responsibility." I knotted my hands in my lap. "This conversation . . . it stays between us?"

"You want it to?"

"Yes."

"Then it will. I keep secrets well enough." Smoke billowed from his lips and curled round his face. "You remind me of someone, and for that I'll grant you a favor. This time. What do you seek?"

"Knowledge about water sprites. Has Milburn been troubled by them often, between the river and the Crossing?"

"We had our share back in the day, or so it's said." He gripped the arms of his chair with gnarled hands. "When I was a lad, there was an outbreak of drownings attributed to the sprites, but there's no knowing for certain, since those who hear their songs don't often live to tell the tale—and unless they choose, you'll never see them."

But I had. With the memory, their voices seemed to echo once more in my ears. I wrapped my arms around myself in an attempt to restore warmth. "Then how would someone make a bargain with them?"

"In theory? I suppose if they knew the person had something

they wanted, they might reveal themselves and try to strike a deal."

"But what would they want to bargain for?"

"Difficult to say." He drew long and hard on his pipe. "Territory has significance for them. The nicer the region they claim—and the closer to a Crossing it is—the more renowned the shiver."

Then did that mean the sprites I'd encountered were from a lesser shiver? For mortals, Milburn was perilously close to Morven Crossing, but the river traveled through the Crossing itself. Surely the part of the river within the Crossing would be more desirable, unless the sprites weren't powerful enough to claim it.

Mr. Heard continued. "From what we know, they're concerned with their status and raising it among their kind. The Otherworld runs on power. Those as don't have it soon die out."

So if I found them better territory, could they be persuaded to leave, despite their bargain? And how could I manage . . . oh. My stomach gave an uncomfortable lurch. The Ashe River ran through Thornhaven. Dared I offer them a home within our inheritance from Mother? It was close to a Crossing, closer than the mill, which occupied the far side of Milburn.

Mr. Heard still spoke, but his words formed a vague rumble in the background as my thoughts raced along this new path.

"Miss Jessa?"

"I beg your pardon. What did you say?"

"Young folks." He huffed. "I said I don't believe sprites and other low fae respond to the same wards as the high fae. Course, that's speculation, but people lump all the Otherfolk together when in fact they're not at all alike. If you were speaking of dealings with a high fae, with power enough to shake our world, then I'd tell you to flee and count yourself fortunate if you escaped the encounter without finding yourself enslaved or killed, though they do favor toying with their prey. But low fae . . . aye, they have powers beyond our ken, but it's possible that you might come out of an encounter unscathed. Still, though sprites may not have all the abilities of high fae, they're plenty strong enough to drag you to the depths. And I won't have you seeking them thinking that pendant will offer protection."

"I know there are risks."

"You think you know." He clenched his pipe, fingers whitening. "Most often, mortal dealings with fae go terribly wrong—and not for the Otherfolk."

"I understand." But what choice did I have?

"Maybe you do, maybe you don't. But I won't let you go without warning." Mr. Heard proceeded to spin tales of horrors that rooted me to my chair—of mortals forced to dance until their feet were blistered and bloodied and beyond, until their very hearts at last gave out; of those compelled to slice their own flesh to ribbons at the bidding of the fae, for their entertainment; of individuals who begged and pleaded for death but were granted no such reprieve.

A rap sounded at the door, and I startled, my heart hammering as though the high fae stormed through the Crossing to batter down the door and take me captive.

But it was only his niece, announcing luncheon. "Will you be staying, Miss Jessa?"

The specters drawn by his words had erased my appetite altogether. I fixed my gaze on the prominent ward-sign etched into the mantel. I was safe here, at least. "Thank you, but I need to return to my aunt."

He waved her out and then regarded me. "It's not too late to change course."

"For me, it is." I lifted my chin. "Why would you share those dreadful stories?"

"So you can choose with full knowledge. Not everyone gets that privilege," he said. "And if you can only see what they want you to see, you'll lose every time."

What could I say to that? Warmth crept up my neck into my cheeks.

He gave me a long, searching look. "But maybe you see more."

"I don't know what you're talking about." But my protest emerged weak and unconvincing.

"So you say. Perhaps you have what you need. But will you use it?" He didn't wait for an answer, but heaved himself upright. "I ask one thing in return for our visit today. If you survive your encounter, you come back afterward and tell me what happened."

"I . . . I'll share what I can." I refused to promise more. I stumbled from the house with my head spinning. I'd gained an idea of how to approach the sprites, but revealed far more than I had planned in the process.

Still, the path before me unfolded with devastating clarity. I'd learned what I could, but to discover the truth about their bargain and attempt to strike a better deal, I'd have to confront them. And despite the confidence I'd assumed with Mr. Heard, I knew it was a dreadful risk.

COME MORNING, I'd gathered my courage to ask Aunt Caris if we could pay another call at the mill, when loud voices drifted in from the corridor.

I peeped out the door, glad for an excuse to postpone my venture.

In the hall, Melle stood arguing with Mrs. Wilkins, the rest of her family ranged about her like kits around a particularly scrappy fox.

Dread wrapped me in its coils. If they were here, something must have gone terribly wrong.

Mrs. Wilkins folded her arms across her ample chest. "If you'll wait, as is proper, I'll check if the ladies wish to receive you."

"I'm telling you—they'll receive me," Melle snapped.

I stepped into the corridor, drawing up to my full, unimpressive height. "Thank you, Mrs. Wilkins. We'd welcome a call."

Muttering under her breath about undesirables and unwelcome dangers, Mrs. Wilkins withdrew, and I beckoned the family into our sitting room.

Jade glared down at the intruders from her perch on the table, and this time, even Essie didn't ask to pet her.

Aunt Caris stood warily in the center of the room. "Have you changed your mind about my offer?"

Melle's shoulders sagged. "I have. Mind you, it doesn't release you from our other agreement."

I ducked my head to hide the surge of frustration. Aunt Caris had done nothing but try to help, and still Melle attempted to coerce her.

The children watched them, wide-eyed. I offered them some blank paper and pencils, and they fell to drawing with more enthusiasm than talent. At least it distracted them from the adult conversation—or so I hoped.

"Did something else happen?" Aunt Caris asked.

"Last night, water rose from the sinkhole and flooded the

cottage." Fresh lines seamed Melle's face. "Most everything in the house is damaged."

Blight and rot. Her words hit like a slap to the face. We'd chosen to wait, to avoid the Vigil, and now this. I stilled a tremor. "Water doesn't flow out of sinkholes, not in the ordinary way of things."

"It's true."

"And you still wish to handle matters without involving . . . anyone else?"

"Aye." The ferocity in her tone cut deep. "It's a course that must be held."

Over in the corner, Aebbe exclaimed over Essie's drawing, and the little girl clambered onto her lap, while Isuel stroked Daw's hair, and Jan continued to draw. They'd already lost so much. This had to end, before they suffered worse.

A soft tap echoed from the other room. Then another. Now a third. I withdrew into the bedchamber, following the sound. In the branches of the tremendous oak that grew outside the window, Nelda perched. She tapped again on the glass, gesticulating frantically. I closed the door, then slid the window open.

"Nelda, where in the Crossings have you been?" I assisted her over the sill.

She looked worse than ever, her dress torn in several places as if by thorns or briars, the bandage on her hand begrimed, and her eyes sunken deep into her head. Had she slept or eaten since she'd fled the inn?

She clung to me. "Please don't let them take me! They have the dogs out, and I only just escaped. The stratesman—he's going to catch me, and I can't go to the madhouse or to the Vigil. I can't."

I lowered my voice further. "If they're using dogs, they'll soon find you here."

"But you can protect me! You're a proper lady. They'll listen to you. Not me. I'm nobody, and nobody's to care if they take me. Except you. You said you cared. Do you?" She clasped my arm, her nails digging into my skin.

"Of course." I led her to the divan. "And I know you're innocent. I'll do my best to convince Stratesman Bancroft of it."

If I came right out and announced to him that water sprites were responsible, he'd call the Vigil for certain—most likely to haul me away alongside Nelda, rather than to investigate the mill. But perhaps if I dropped a hint, it might cause him to consider new lines of inquiry. Regardless, I *couldn't* let him take Nelda.

I rubbed the icy knot in my chest.

A low murmur of voices issued from the other room, one of them male. Were we out of time?

Above the rest, Aunt Caris's voice rose. "I'm certain she knows nothing, but if you insist . . ."

At that moment, the door flung wide. Aunt Caris stood on the threshold, Stratesman Bancroft behind her, and beyond them, Melle and her family, all motionless.

My stomach hollowed. Now to give an account, one that revealed neither too much nor too little. Could I manage it?

CHAPTER 10

"Miss Jessa, I thought I made myself clear." Stratesman Bancroft bristled like an angry bulldog. "Yet you chose to harbor a dangerous fugitive in defiance of law and sense alike."

I wanted to melt through the floorboards and vanish, but I forced myself to remain and shield Nelda. "I assure you, I mean no defiance of the law. She only returned moments ago, and I was attempting to determine what happened in her absence."

"It's not your place to question her, but to follow the rule of law."

I folded my hands in front of my waist and sought an even tone, one that would not betray my fears. "Mr. Bancroft, do I look like a criminal? I desire to see justice prevail, and that's precisely why I wished to speak with Nelda."

"You shouldn't have—"

"Besides which, I'm certain she's innocent." If I let him continue to chastise, I might never find the courage to go on.

"She ran away, went into hiding. Hardly the actions of an innocent woman."

Behind me, Nelda drew a ragged breath.

"She's alone and afraid, with an entire town ranged against her. Of course she fled." The great oak rustled beyond the open window, its stalwart and encouraging presence a welcome contrast to the hostility within the room. I pressed onward. "I want to find the culprit as well, since my aunt and I have committed to stay and aid Melle until matters are resolved. But arresting the wrong person will do nothing to help the situation at the mill—and could cause irreparable harm to any number of reputations, including your own."

Aunt Caris clutched at her ward-pendant, a quick inhale revealing her disapproval. A sinking sensation hollowed my stomach. A proper young lady remained demure, respectful of authorities and of her elders. She didn't brashly challenge them, denounce their actions, and cast aspersions on their motives. Doubtless, Aunt Caris would have something to say about my behavior later.

But with the knowledge I held, I couldn't turn back. I inhaled the soft green fragrance of the new leaves on the old oak, and somehow, it steadied me.

Meanwhile, Stratesman Bancroft remained silent—perhaps as shocked as Aunt Caris—and on instinct, I pressed this line of argument further. "In fact, there are those who might say you arrested a vulnerable young woman because she was an easy mark, with none to defend her."

"I would never—" He cleared his throat. "All evidence points to her."

"All evidence. Truly?" I pressed on, despite the way my head throbbed with the pressure of disapproval on all sides. "There's no way Nelda could have caused flooding from the sinkhole, much less have created it. How do you explain its presence and apparent defiance of natural laws?"

He rubbed his beard, looking as though the shaft had struck home. "That's for the Magister to sort out."

I turned over what I knew of Stratesman Bancroft in my mind. The suggestion of damage to his reputation appeared to impact him a great deal. Certainly his advancement in his vocation would depend upon impressing his superiors. I inclined my head. "Will the Magister look favorably upon a case that wastes his time? What if you take Nelda in and the attacks continue? Isn't it worth considering the alternative first?"

"What alternative would that be?" His tone was less hostile, more open.

How could I broach this without breaking trust—and condemning myself along with Aebbe? I ventured forward with care. "You must admit there have been some peculiarities about the situation at the mill, ones that mortal involvement can't easily explain. Perhaps they seem common to those of you who dwell in Milburn, but it did rouse me to wonder."

His brows rose, bristling with disapproval once more—for ladies should not express curiosity on such matters. Nevertheless, I forged onward, careful to avoid looking at Aunt Caris. Her displeasure would pierce far deeper.

"I paid a call on Mr. Heard yesterday so I might more readily understand what sort of fae activity is common in Milburn. Some of his tales of the Otherkind reminded me of what's happened at the mill. This close to Morven Crossing, isn't it possible they could be responsible?"

"Otherkind?" His voice deepened. "I suppose they *could* have a hand in it, but why? What cause would they have to sabotage the mill?"

"Who can understand their ways?" I shrugged. "But when Melle told us this morning of the uncharacteristic behavior of the sinkhole—either someone involved has the resources to countermand the natural order by alchemy, or the Otherkind must play some part."

Melle looked grim, but she could hardly protest in front of a roomful of people. No matter which way I turned, I earned someone's displeasure. Oh, I wanted to flee back to Avons, to the peace of my glasshouse, away from the glares and glowers. Uncomfortable heat prickled up my face as I awaited his response.

"Otherkind." He stroked his beard again. "I'll admit I didn't consider their involvement. We've had our troubles in the past but nothing like this, least to my knowledge. If they're involved, this would be a Vigil matter."

"Surely there's no need for that yet." I put the weight of my fears behind my words, twisting them into a plea that rose from somewhere deep within. Once more, that discomfiting sensation crept over me, shading my voice with an unfamiliar tone. "Wouldn't it be better to make certain before you call in the Vigil? I imagine the Magister would favor thorough work, and a closer examination of the sinkhole could reveal if any human device caused the damage."

He nodded slowly. "I suppose that's reasonable."

As much as I'd willed it, his capitulation surprised me. A tiny bit of the tension within unwound.

Then Stratesman Bancroft's gaze flicked to Nelda. "Room for doubt aside, I can't leave her to roam Milburn, not after all that's happened."

"Can't she stay at the inn? Under guard, if you deem it necessary?" I took Nelda's hand in mine and gave it a gentle squeeze, hoping she would not flee or protest. "Then, if another attack occurs, it'll be quite clear whether or not she was involved."

"Very well." His eyes narrowed. "But if what I find points the finger at her, I want no more argument when I take her in."

I bowed my head. "It will be as you say."

It would never come to that, however, for I would confront the sprites this afternoon—come what may.

But Aunt Caris refused to release me so readily. She pressed me into service, asking for my assistance settling Melle and her family into another set of rooms at the inn. Once we'd finally returned to our own chambers, she closed the door and turned to me, cheeks flushed and indignation high.

"What were you thinking, Jessa?" She crossed to the still-open window and slammed it shut. "To defy a stratesman and argue before him like a barrister? It's not our responsibility to see that he arrests the right individual. And to stir up rumors of the Otherkind? You might as well have lobbed a hornet's nest into the room. You of all people should know better."

My eyes burned. "I'm sorry, Aunt Caris. It's only that Nelda has no one else to stand up for her."

And I was sure of her innocence, though I couldn't confess the reason to Aunt Caris. But perhaps the suspicion had already entered her mind. She and Father had always sought to protect me from whatever was bent inside me, and the mention of Otherkind likely rekindled her fears. I lowered my gaze, unwilling to see the disappointment on her face.

After a moment, she sighed softly. "Yes, well, it's done now. Perhaps it's my fault as much as yours for bringing you into this situation in the first place."

"It's not your fault." The flaw rested within me, not Aunt Caris.

"I have a responsibility to you and to your father." Her lips trembled slightly. "I want your word you'll not argue with the stratesman any further, nor seek to get the Vigil involved."

That I could promise, and it appeared to ease her fears, for if she had any inkling of my plans, she'd have locked me in my bedchamber and buried the key.

But she did not, and when she departed to visit the bakery, I made my excuses, claiming a desire to ramble and sketch—and truly, my fingers ached to hold a pencil and capture some of the lovely wildflowers along the way. But I didn't have the time.

Not till I'd seen the sprites.

Jade prowled the road alongside me, always keeping pace— more akin to a dog than a cat in her close companionship. I only hoped it didn't falter when the first tempting bird or chipmunk crossed our path, though I'd come to have more faith in her unusual constancy with each passing day and to rely on it, perhaps more than I should.

The playful breeze tugged at my skirts and swept over the violets that carpeted the bank along the road. Their essence drifted forth, sweetly reassuring. I fought the allure, though the effort sent a spasm of pain down my neck. The protection I'd taken for granted before now came only with great difficulty. Every wisp of errant sensation, sound, or scent I stuffed deep into the cage at the back of my mind and bound within. With each step, I wove the vines tighter. Never mind that it felt like suffocating my own soul, I refused to see or hear anything out of the ordinary.

With so much at stake, I could afford no distraction, whether it sprang from undue influence of my own emotions or the Crossing. At all costs, I must retain clarity of thought. How else could I hope to survive a negotiation with the sprites?

Jade chuffed and shook her head.

Though I managed at last to quiet the plants, I couldn't purge Mr. Heard's tales from my mind, nor the stark reality of the death Nelda's father suffered at the hands of the sprites, imprisoned beneath the surface of the waters. Had the allure of their song broken when his lungs started to burn, when the need for air forced him to inhale and the waters rushed into his lungs, cold and smothering? Had terror paralyzed his muscles, or had he thrashed against his captors? Had he realized the fate he'd brought upon himself?

He wasn't alive to ask. And I didn't want to know the answers, not truly. With each dreadful image, my steps slowed. I almost turned back. But if I did, what then? Aunt Caris, with her insistence on remaining in Milburn, would be vulnerable to their wiles, as would Melle, Isuel, and the children—who'd done nothing to deserve their suffering. Not to mention what I risked, if I remained here with them.

As I approached the mill, clouds obscured the sun, and the day grew more chill, like the deeps of the river. One misstep, and I would experience the cold waters myself. I wrapped my shawl tighter around my shoulders, its warmth insufficient to chase away the icy fear within. Perhaps Mr. Heard was right. Perhaps I would pay a tremendous penalty for attempting to deal with the Otherworld.

But what other path remained?

I bypassed the cottage and its flooded yard, taking the path that led to the weir. Perhaps they favored that location, but if not, I'd force myself to walk the banks until I found them.

I paused alongside the willows, and their branches stirred in the wind, bending toward me. After a moment, I pressed past them to stand at the bank of the river. The current flowed steadily, burbling over the weir, but I perceived nothing of note.

The sun on the water strengthened, and my vision blurred.

Slight ripples formed on the river, as if fish kissed the surface, and the melody of its movement sank into my senses.

Jade gave a low-pitched growl and twined around my ankles, barring forward motion. I tucked her into my arms as the song soaked deeper, soothing my frayed soul.

The knots within loosened.

The clouds withdrew further, and the sun beat hot on my shoulders. And oh, I craved the coolness of the waters, the refreshment they promised. The river murmured assurances of serenity, of the sweetness of surrender.

Tension ebbed from my body as I eased forward, picking my way among the reeds at the edge. The soft susurration of the waters formed a song far more soul-stirring than even the finest orchestral performance. It spoke of peace and play, rest and respite, laughter and love.

And I drank it in, the music sating a deep thirst. Everything faded as the allure of the river filled my senses. Then a sharp pain pierced my arm, and I stumbled.

Jade.

She sank her claws deeper into my skin, her green eyes narrow, glowing slits. I gasped.

Instantly, she retracted her claws.

The vines on my cage of thorns snapped, and a flood of sensation swept over me. Frigid water rushed around my legs, sending pinpricks across my skin. I tried to still my forward motion and instead stumbled over a slick stone, nearly upending in the river. But the same force that compelled me onward also kept me from falling—the sprites.

They surrounded me, forcing me farther from the shore, their unnaturally beautiful faces a breath away, close enough to reveal cold pleasure in their eyes, which changed hue from one moment to the next, just like the river itself.

How had they ensnared me?

A wild, brackish aroma emanated from them, carrying the energy of the river and an edge of malice. My lungs constricted as the odor swirled around me.

I attempted to plant my feet, but they wrenched me onward. Never mind how they'd lured me into the waters—I must get free. Unless I wanted to become like the miller.

This time, I tried to pull out of their grasp. But as if I'd no more strength than a babe, they ignored my efforts, yanking at my skirts with claw-tipped fingers sharp as jagged shells, rending my gown, forcing me deeper into the currents. The river reached my waist, churning wildly about me. My throat burned as if the waters already forced their way inside.

Gently.

Don't rush her.

Between the words laced a relentless song from the sprites who frolicked in the river, their diaphanous garments sparkling in the sun like foam on the waters. They issued a call to join them at their play and find rest. But it no longer allured. Instead, it chilled me to the core.

Come, pretty lady.

This one will be fun. Not like old miller.

Don't pull so hard. We don't want it to end too soon.

Their play meant my death. Meant my body, pulled to the depths, my lungs contracting, gasping for air, burning with pain as they frolicked around me. I braced my feet in the muck of the riverbed, straining against their grasping hands.

But one tug from the tallest sprite, and I stumbled forward once more, the waters surging up to my chest.

They were too many, too strong.

The world spun around me, a blur of silver and blue, nothing steady to grasp, nowhere safe to turn.

From her perch on my shoulders, Jade snarled, her teeth bared. Her weight increased. One of the sprites raised its hand toward her, webbed fingers clenched around a gleaming silvery blade.

No, not Jade. A wave of heat swept over me, that unfamiliar note creeping into my voice, as if the Otherness of Milburn poured through me. "Release us."

A chittering of shock swept through their ranks. The fists tangled in my clothing slackened, and I broke away, charging for the shore, my soaked skirts tangling about my legs and impeding my movements, every step a battle.

The shell-sharp nails of a sprite raked my arm, and I shoved it with all my might. Jade hissed in the face of another, slashing her claws along its eyes.

It fell back with a cry. The waters churned furiously, and I lost my footing. Muck and mire tugged at my feet, unwilling to release, as though the sprites used even the elements against me. Perhaps they did.

My heart drummed against the wall of my chest, and sweat slicked my neck. Cold as death, the river numbed my legs, made my movements slow and clumsy. The sprites circled closer, laughing and singing once more, their pale-blue forms flicking in and out of sight among the waters.

This one entertains.

Never mind my efforts, they knew there would be no escape. Still I swept my hands through the water, seeking deliverance.

My fingers twined around a strong willow bough. I stretched and grasped another. Vibrant green strength quickened within me, and I surged into the shallows.

The sprites backed away from the lashing willow branches, which whipped the surface of the waters. I stumbled onto shore, my gown drenched and muscles quivering. I'd come so close, too close to sharing the fate of the miller. I pulled in a shuddering breath as the spring wind sliced through my wet garments, then staggered away from the bank. I must distance myself before they found a way to lure me back in.

With Jade at my side, I stumbled down the weir path . . . away from the sprites, away from my failure.

CHAPTER 11

Somehow, I made it back to the inn, my defeat as bitter as wormwood in my mouth. At least I had escaped alive, unlike many before me. Yet cold seeped through my soaked clothes, piercing so deep I felt as though I'd never be warm again. Jade marched beside me, her constancy unbroken even by the passage of a chittering sparrow. Her proud walk indicated she shared none of my shame—nor should she, for her actions had preserved my life.

She'd made no mistakes.

Though I kept to the shadows as I walked through Milburn, avoiding the attention of curious townsfolk, I couldn't escape notice once inside the White Hart. Someone always kept an eye on the welcoming room, and this afternoon, it was Mrs. Wilkins, who exclaimed her dismay at my bedraggled appearance.

Through chattering teeth, I told her I'd taken a tumble into the river, and she fussed over me much as Aunt Caris would have. Mrs. Wilkins insisted I take a hot bath and afterward plied me with tea.

Once I escaped her ministrations, I collapsed into bed, exhausted and still cold to the core. I piled up every blanket I could find and then curled into the middle of the nest, shielding myself from the outside world. But I could not shield myself from the truth, from the relentless logic breaking down the fragile hope I held that Father had been right about my lifelong struggle, that my experiences in Milburn had been only the influence exerted by a nearby Crossing and strained emotions.

If I'd perceived the sprites the first time through an undue influence of the Crossing, I'd not have been able to block them from sight by attempting to exert control over my . . . fae-touch. For it could be nothing else—I'd perceived them only when Jade had jolted my inner cage open, exposing the fault within, a fault which by all accounts allowed its bearer to see through the glamours of the low fae.

Jade leapt upon the bed and stretched her body across mine, nuzzling my chin and offering comfort I did not deserve.

I turned from her and buried my face deep in the pillow, yet I could not block out the vivid forms of the sprites. Their stark, cruel beauty remained etched on my mind, a bleak reminder of the fate before me.

I might have succeeded in controlling the fae-touch for a time, but its influence was growing, along with the looming threat of madness. My inner taint didn't emerge from emotional strain as Father claimed, rather it was grafted into my being like a scion into rootstock, forever changing the plant as it matured. Perhaps Milburn had allowed the fae-touch to strengthen more rapidly, but I must admit the town appeared to influence none of its other inhabitants unduly. Certainly, Aunt Caris experienced nothing of the sort.

My eyes burned, and I wound myself tighter in the cocoon of blankets. Oh, how could I bear it? I didn't want to think about what had happened at the river, didn't want to consider any further what it meant. So I shut everything out and slowly sank into the peculiar state between sleeping and waking. I drifted in a gray haze as the sun sank lower on the horizon. The door to the sitting room remained ajar, and after a time, voices dispersed the fog that hung over me.

I blinked into the dimness.

"How can I make you understand?" A note of sharp distress from Aunt Caris roused me fully. "I've tried everything. *Everything*. I simply don't have the resources to purchase the other mill, and no one I know will risk their capital on such a chancy venture."

"Have you asked your brother? Surely he would pay to keep your past hidden, if he knew."

So Melle was blackmailing Aunt Caris. At once, my nest of blankets became stifling. I pressed myself upright, shoving the quilts aside.

"You don't know Alden." Her voice was rueful. "My brother thinks only of his studies since Kensa passed. He cares nothing for society and their views. It's up to me to plan for the family, my nieces and their futures. Please, Melle, you must see reason."

What should I do? To listen in on another's conversation was a hallmark of ill breeding, but I was trapped in the bedchamber. If I interrupted, I might raise both their ire.

"You think of your nieces, but I have to consider my own family."

"Consider your family, yes. But must that mean extortion?" A scraping sound echoed through the room, as if someone had moved a chair. "What happened to you? The woman I remember, the woman who was my friend, would never have stooped so low."

"The woman you remember is gone! She was buried with her

husband. You're worried about the future of your nieces, about seeing them well-wed and situated in society. But I must worry about keeping those who depend on me from poverty and starvation."

"Then perhaps . . . with more time . . ." There was a faint shuffling. "I don't see any way to purchase the mill, but I could help in other ways, if only you would acknowledge them, if only you would stop these threats. Then we could proceed in friendship, as we once did. Alden might permit you to stay with us, for a bit, and maybe I could find some sort of position that would allow your family to remain together—"

"Might. Perhaps. Maybe. You ask me to gamble with everyone I love on the chance you *might* secure us a future."

"I offer all I have," Aunt Caris said. "Can't you trust me, trust our friendship?"

"What friendship can remain, after I've threatened to share your letters with the world?" Melle's voice lost its harsh edge, became low and pained.

A long pause, then at last Aunt Caris spoke. "I've learned to release the past and look to a better future. I must, every day, else the pain of it would cripple me. Can you?"

"Oh, Caris. What have I done? What will we do?" Suddenly Melle began to weep, a broken sound I never dreamed of hearing from such an intimidating woman. "I never meant you harm, but I'm so afraid . . ."

Their pain ripped at me, stinging my eyes with unshed tears, even as their voices softened, and Aunt Caris whispered words of comfort to Melle. I sank back onto the bed.

When Jade stalked across the coverlet and planted herself on my lap, I no longer attempted to withdraw, but tugged her close. Somehow, Melle found courage to give up her attempt to control Aunt Caris. Somehow, Aunt Caris found courage to forgive. And somehow, I must find courage to return to the mill.

And this time, I must embrace this fae-touch, must welcome the frightening flood of sensation, the invasion of the Otherworld into my soul, so that I might confront them properly—not vulnerable to their wiles, but as one who understood their words and perceived their form. My determination to believe I experienced only emotional aberrations I must shut down had nearly gotten me killed this afternoon. But if I surrendered, if I allowed the force of fae-touch I'd battled my entire life to shape my perception, would I ever be able to eradicate its influence? Or would I fall deeper into its grasp until I lost myself forever and became like Mrs. Murton, a danger to others in my madness, only worthy of the Institutions?

I bit my lip and tasted the salt-tang of blood.

I refused to shrink back, no matter the risk. I'd bound it before, kept it locked it deep inside. Surely I could do it again, even if Father's explanation was a lie. I could, and I would. Once we left Milburn and returned to Avons, I would bind the fae-touch to protect myself and those I loved, and take up my role as a proper daughter once more.

If I possessed the strength.

Over breakfast, Melle and Aunt Caris discussed possible paths for the future of the Hopkins family. Given their limited options, it was no wonder Melle had thought of nothing but pressing Aunt Caris for the other mill. Hearing their lack of progress toward a solution strengthened my resolve—and how it needed bolstering, after a night spent reliving the terror of my near-drowning. Twice, I'd woken gasping for air, my lungs convinced they were seared by the waters.

But Mr. Heard had suggested if I could see true, if I could keep them from controlling my perception, perhaps I could negotiate with them. With that expectation to gird me, I would return.

I only hoped he was right.

Absorbed in conversation, Aunt Caris scarcely took note when I murmured an excuse for my departure. I fought a pang of guilt. She allowed such liberties because I'd never outwardly strayed from proprieties before. If she knew my intent . . .

I shook my head and lifted the reins of the hired curricle. Jade curled atop my feet, her presence soothing. I leaned down and stroked her head, and she *mrowed* softly. As we traveled through Milburn, I startled at every gleam of light through the tree boughs, as though the sprites could leave the waters and stalk me through the forest. But worse than facing the sprites, when I reached the river, I would have to allow the fae-touch to surface. What would happen then?

What if I risked everything, and it still wasn't enough?

I sat up straighter. If there was another way, one less costly, no amount of reflection had revealed it. And no matter where I fled, I could never escape myself.

At the cottage, we abandoned the carriage and continued on foot. When we approached the river, a ruff of fur rose along Jade's back. I drew in a breath, and when I exhaled, I imagined the thorned vines untangling, their tight weave opening ever so slightly. It came on prickling and painful, a tide of feeling that threatened to unmoor me, even as I wrestled to keep myself anchored. I wrapped my arms around my middle. What was I doing? Father had warned me countless times against the danger of this taint—even without knowing it as fae-touch. If he knew . . . if Aunt Caris knew . . . but they were not here, only whispers fast becoming a full-voiced chorus around me.

My whole body trembled as I wrestled to quiet the onslaught—fragrances, sounds, feelings altogether too *alive* to belong to this world—to push down the sensations without locking them away altogether. I pressed my hand against the bark of the nearest willow, until the knobbled ridges dug into my skin, the mundane, familiar touch clearing my mind. A vibrant strength coursed through my veins, checking the tide. I allowed myself to sag against the trunk of the tree, its steady pulse fortifying me.

And it seemed as if the pulse contained words: *they come, they come, they come.*

I turned to the river. Its waters rushed merrily over the weir in endless succession. But then a ripple formed near the center, followed by another. One after the other, sprites surged to the surface, their lithe forms gleaming and powerful, their beauty as striking as their cruelty.

She's come back to play.

A chortle of glee. *Today, we keep her.*

My skin prickled as though their shell-sharp claws already raked across it, but I forced myself to remain still. "I can hear you, and I've come to talk."

A murmur of surprise swept their ranks.

Yes, you shall come. Come and play, pretty one.

A weedy-haired sprite reared from the surface, his torso glimmering silver-blue like the belly of a fish. *Lovely lady, the waters wish to greet you. They bring peace. You must come.*

Lovely lady come.

Their voices merged with the rushing waters of the river, persuasive despite the absurdity of their words. My blood thrummed with a desire to feel the caress of the waters on my skin. I stepped forward, brushing against river reeds and rushes.

They scratched through the fabric of my skirt, and their staid fortitude straightened my spine, urging me to project a certainty I did not feel. I halted within a cluster of reeds, as though they could protect me should the sprites decide to wield the waters as a weapon. "I want to make a bargain."

Silence met my demand. Then a cackle of delight.

A bargain, my pretty?

A slim female curved her dark lips in a twisted smile that somehow diminished none of the perfect symmetry of her face. *She wishes to make a bargain. What fun we shall have!*

The tall male surged forward, ripples spreading in his wake. *A bargain it shall be. What have you to offer?*

Their eagerness sent a shiver down my spine, as though the icy waters crept once more up my limbs, ready to claim my life. If I failed to craft a proper bargain, nothing could save me from their cruel whims. But at least the inducement I dangled before them brought me momentary safety, since they appeared to expect an entertaining offer. I concealed my hands in the folds of my skirt, lest their trembling betray me. "If you wish to bargain, first tell me: by what authority do you seek to drive away the current owners of the mill?"

The sprites had referred to it as their right, and before I attempted to remedy the situation, I must understand.

Ooh, she wants to hear the other bargain. A sprite with pale-blue hair and dark eyes grinned, sharp teeth glinting white.

Shall we tell? another asked.

Yes, yes. She will see our brilliance.

Then we shall bargain again. More and better. The slim female flipped through the water, her lithe figure shimmering in and out of view.

The tall male—perhaps their leader?—took charge of the

conversation, quieting the rest. *We bargained with old miller for new home.*

"A new home? What of your old one?"

Rusalka drove us away.

Rusalka? Water-dwellers like these sprites, rusalkas were low fae—yet their power came closer to that of the high fae, and they were known for striking without mercy, their beautiful feminine forms concealing great strength and ruthless cunning. I ran my fingers across the bulrushes, their thick, green stalks rasping over my skin. "So why did you bargain with the miller?"

His mill and weir imprison the river. The waters wish to flow free. As do we.

Murmurs of disgust. They churned about angrily.

Without mortal bonds, this spot would be perfect. Banks of willow and river oaks with roots for homes, deeps to play. But not in chains. So we watch. We wait. We play with the weir till waters flow through.

A chuckle. *Miller was angry. When he came to fix weir, he dropped in his watch.*

The weedy sprite smirked. *Too much drink, old man had.*

Ha! Fumble fingers. The slim female mimed the action.

Pretty watch it was, all gold, said another.

We might have kept it, but better to bargain. The leader spoke over the others. *So we offer: he abandons mill and weir and frees river, we return watch.*

"He agreed to give you his livelihood in exchange for his watch?" Fae could not lie, though they could twist truth to deceive, but their words seemed straightforward. Whatever his reasons, the miller must have bound himself to them. What could have possibly possessed him? Unless he had no intention of keeping his word. Perhaps he believed the sprites unable to enforce the agreement. If so, he could have promised anything without the intent to follow through.

He swore, a binding bargain. We gave watch; he broke word. So we sang him into the waters. His daughter, she should have kept oath. But she did not, only ran away, though she has paid. Then new lady. She thinks she can break bargain also. Mortal fools, all. The leader rose further, his broad torso gleaming in the sunlight. *Bargains cannot be broken. Mill and river and weir all ours.*

So they tormented Nelda and Melle because of a bargain struck by the old miller, even after his death? Small wonder Nelda appeared so haunted, and with the suspicions of the townsfolk against her, she'd not dare confess any encounter she endured. Jade nudged my ankle, and I lifted her into my arms. "But . . . but Melle made no pact with you."

Matters not. Mill and weir and river already ours.

That idea seemed firmly implanted. I could argue with them all day long and achieve nothing. No mortal law bound them. But they wanted a home, a place of freedom and safety. Which left Thornhaven, however much the notion galled. "What if I offered you another home—a better one?"

Why should we leave?

"Because the mortals don't understand your agreement. They'll continue to sell the mill or try to repair it, and they'll never leave you in peace. They'll never respect your claim."

Then we shall drive them forth. They will fear. And they will go.

"Perhaps they will fear, but it will move them to call in the Vigil, who will seek to evict you with any means at their disposal."

An uneasy murmur.

The leader glowered. *Let them try. We fear not your Vigil.*

"But the longer you engage in open conflict, the greater the chances you'll draw attention from the high fae." It was guesswork, harkening back to what I'd overheard from them earlier, but it appeared to make an impact.

They sank lower in the waters, whispering among themselves.

I hugged Jade closer. "At least consider what I have to offer."

Alongside Thornhaven, the Ashe River wended into a large lake, with a narrow tree-covered island near the center. Surely it would be an appealing prospect for relocation. Though I deplored their cruel dealings with mortals, I sympathized with a desire for home and safe haven, which made this concession easier to grant. If only I could confide all in Ada and Ainslie and gain their agreement first. Given that they were older than I, it should be their right.

Yet Mother had left Thornhaven to us jointly, and though there might be substantial differences in personality and inclination between us, in this, I knew Ada and Ainslie as well as myself. Aunt Caris had become a mother to us, and no sacrifice would be too great to protect her. I chose my words with care. "My sisters and I have a property near Aelfgard Crossing. There are few mortals there, which means no towns, no mills or weirs, little human traffic of any kind on the waters. Would you make your home there?"

They turned to one another.

Mortals may come, try to claim.

It matters not, if it belongs to us.

But does she have rights to bargain?

"I do, but I will only grant you the right to inhabit the waters. You're not to interfere with mortals, nor sing them your songs, nor play with them, nor are you to harm my family or any we give leave to dwell on or maintain the land."

Why should we lose our play?

"To gain peace." In my arms, Jade's warmth reassured. "You

may do what you please among your own kind. Entertain yourselves with them. For my part, I give you my word that if we enter an agreement, our portion of the lake and river will remain untouched, never dammed or obstructed, as long as my sisters and I retain ownership."

How would I ever explain this to Ada and Ainslie? I knew they would agree, for Aunt Caris's sake, and for the other innocents caught in this trap. But to confess all to them . . . I shuddered.

Thoughtful murmurs swirled through the waters.

I'd best press the point. "Besides, if you're driven from here, if the rusalka expand their territory or Melle involves the Vigil, you'll end up with nowhere to dwell. If you stay, it's a gamble. Perhaps you gain greater entertainment—but perhaps you end up with nothing." I then wove for them a description from my childhood memories of Thornhaven, of the beauties and joys I experienced in our weeks spent there. "Wouldn't territory so lovely and so near Aelfgard Crossing gain you renown?"

There was a long silence, then the leader swam closer. *You speak for mortals. What if rusalka or other fae-kind lay claim to Aelfgard waters? New home does no good then.*

We were close, so close. I sensed it, and my pulse thrummed in anticipation, a rhythm that matched the rustle of the willow leaves. I fought the urge to lock away the errant sensations. Dared I give my word on this? "If other fae-kind try to assert a claim, I'll do all in my power to remove them."

Place your hand in the water.

What in the Crossings? I glanced at Jade. Her tail thrashed and twitched, but she made no attempt to resist as I lowered her to the ground. Dared I approach? Could I trust the near-bargain, as yet unsealed? If I did not, I gained nothing from the risks I'd taken already.

A faint drumming in my ears, I crept forward and rested my palm on the surface of the river. Something pricked my hand, and I flinched. A bead of blood fell from my skin onto the surface of the water, which swirled beneath the impact.

Hmm. Very interesting. Yes. Yes. That is acceptable.

Words bound, not blood . . . so what were they after? I rubbed my stinging palm. "Do we have a bargain, then? You forsake all claim to the river here, the mill and weir, and you reveal yourself as responsible for the sabotage in a time and way of my choosing, making plain your culpability in all that has happened. In exchange, you receive a place where you may live undisturbed—as long as you refrain from interfering with mortals."

Agreed. We are bound.

With that, our fates were sealed. The whispers of the bulrushes took on a cheerier note, their steady song interspersed with bursts of reedy whistling, an unwelcome distraction. Yet I dared not try to restrain the evidence of fae-touch, not yet, not until I witnessed the bargain fulfilled.

As the sun lowered in the sky, we sorted out how the sprites would reveal their presence and act as though alchemical means drove them out, rather than a bargain between us. They appeared to relish the theatricals that awaited and the deceptions it would entail. Among themselves they chortled gleefully, while I did my best to stifle my misgivings. If I'd missed something or left details forgotten, the whole thing could unravel, leaving matters worse than ever.

CHAPTER 12

Early the next morning, Melle visited our rooms. We'd just finished breakfast, and Eda was bustling around, clearing dishes and restoring order. She cast several curious glances into the sitting room, so Melle waited until she departed to speak. "I plan to return to the cottage today. If the water's receded enough, I need to see what's salvageable."

Clouds hung low and gray beyond the old, wavy glass of the windows, heavy with impending rain, and past the sill, the aged oak rustled with anticipation of quenching its thirst. I busied myself rearranging flowers in the nearest vase in an attempt to distract myself from its enthusiasm.

"You can't wait for the weather to clear?" Aunt Caris asked.

"I need to know where we stand, what damage has been done." Melle's gaze drifted toward the dark ribbon of the river, just visible in the distance. "I told Aebbe, Isuel, and the children to remain here."

Aunt Caris adjusted the embroidered pillows on the divan. "You still think there's danger?"

"If Jessa is correct and Nelda's not responsible, then yes. But the stratesman hasn't found anyone else who might have done the damage." Her eyes looked unspeakably weary, and deep shadows gathered beneath them.

"About that . . . I have a confession to make." I attempted to keep my voice steady. "I went to the mill yesterday and walked along the river path to look for any evidence of the saboteur."

Both Aunt Caris and Melle remonstrated me, their words tangling on top of each other.

"Please, I know there was some risk, but I wanted to see if I could find anything Stratesman Bancroft may have missed." I swept the few dead blossoms from the tabletop and into the rubbish bin. Busying my hands helped me conceal the emotions threatening to surge to the surface. "A woman's eye notes more details—"

"Ha! There is that," Melle said.

"And this was too important to be left to chance."

"I wish you hadn't taken such risks, my dear." Aunt Caris sank into the nearest chair. "If you'd stumbled upon the saboteur, you might have been injured."

"I agree with Caris, but it's over and done now, no sense looking back." A spark rekindled in Melle's eyes, banishing the shadows. "Did you find anything?"

"Well, I noticed something . . . odd at the river. There were strange patterns along the banks, like fae-circles." Patterns the sprites had formed at my request. I'd watched in a sort of horrified fascination as the shimmering forms of the sprites had become slightly more solid when they'd emerged from the waters. Once on the river banks, they'd spun in a violent dance, their movements somehow birthing the entwined circles and the peculiar plants that sprung from them—a dazzling display of power. I shook out my shawl and placed it with my hat. "If you're returning to the mill today, we ought to ask the stratesman to accompany us so he can examine them."

"Fae. You're certain?"

"I'm confident that what I saw came from no mortal source."

"Then perhaps Aebbe . . ." She cut off abruptly. "Yes, we'd best inform him. He told us he'd be staying at the White Hart until the matter is settled, so he doesn't have to journey from his home in Harbury so often."

Though Harbury was the nearest town, to travel back and forth took the better part of a day, according to Aunt Caris. No doubt the whole situation tested his patience to the limit, and now he was separated from his family entirely until this was resolved. Not to mention whatever his superiors had to say about the delay—but it would last no longer.

Today, I would reveal the truth.

But would the sprites hold to their word? Had I crafted the bargain well enough? If not, disaster awaited. Striving for calm, I secured my hat, and Jade clambered up to her favorite position, draped like a stole across my shoulders.

Down in the welcoming room, Aunt Caris procured a wagon to fetch any items which might be salvageable from the cottage, while Melle went to find Stratesman Bancroft.

Together, Aunt Caris and I crossed into the courtyard, where the fragrance of sweetlace hung heavy, a joyful herald of the fruits to come. Its celebratory song beckoned, but Jade *mrowed* low in my ear, refocusing me as Stratesman Bancroft and Melle strode across the flagstones. I hoped he would join Melle in the more spacious wagon, but he asked Aunt Caris if he could ride with us in the carriage instead. Though I willed her to decline, she swiftly gave consent.

My skin prickled with a thousand tiny needles as I offered him a greeting. Could I truly carry this off?

"Tell me, Miss Jessa, of the patterns you saw on the banks." Stratesman Bancroft leaned back in the seat and spread his arms, apparently at ease. But his narrowed eyes belied his relaxed stance. "And why do you think they're connected to the sabotage?"

Aunt Caris studied him, an expression of distaste etched across her features. "I didn't accept your company so that you could interrogate my niece."

"My apologies, but she's the only one who noticed anything out of the ordinary. Just as she's the only one to insist on Nelda's innocence. So I must inquire as to how she discovered these patterns."

"It was hardly a discovery." I stroked Jade's soft head, forcing a steadiness I did not feel. "They're quite evident, I assure you. Did you examine the banks by the weir?"

"Aye, but not since the house flooded." The admission came reluctantly. "What did these patterns look like? Melle says they resemble fae-circles?"

I drew out my sketch pad and copied a series of concentric circles and the small plants that had emerged from them following the dance of the sprites, the same Other-infused plants I'd spied beside the sinkhole and the mill itself.

I tore the sheet loose and handed it to him.

"Interesting. I found plants like those growing on the underside of the barn after it flooded. I thought nothing of it then, but if you discovered them on the banks . . . and those circles . . ." He stroked his beard. "Maybe your notion of Otherkind isn't so far-fetched after all. I'll need to examine the evidence myself before calling in the Vigil, of course."

"Of course." The pinpricks returned. If I couldn't convince him to accept our performance, if he summoned the Vigil . . .

"I don't like this at all," said Aunt Caris. "Perhaps we should turn back."

"Melle needs us—she shouldn't face this alone." Was this the moment? I didn't want Stratesman Bancroft to question me closely, so the timing must be perfect. I rummaged in my reticule. "Besides, in case of encounters with fae, I've acquired this."

I lifted a device that resembled a ward-stone, a device alchemists claimed would repel fae. A ward-stone was the simplest and most affordable of their offerings—though still quite costly—and easiest to imitate. Those who put faith in their claims, rather than the more traditional wards of herbalists and wise women, would attach the long, narrow shaft of stone with iron brackets somewhere on the doorframe of their house. Or they might even wear a smaller ward-stone as a brooch or pin.

After striking my bargain with the sprites, I'd found a suitably shaped stone, and once Aunt Caris had retired last night, I'd polished it, then etched and gilded onto its surface the archaic symbols used by the alchemists. I'd mentally thanked Ibbie for her zeal in antiquarian studies, which had given me a passing acquaintance with their runes, a resurrection of a language of old. My imitation ward-stone contained none of whatever hidden processes the alchemists used, but from the outside, one would never know. Not unless Stratesman Bancroft sought an alchemist—but given the time and expense involved, I doubted he'd engage one.

Stratesman Bancroft raised a brow, looking impressed rather than dubious. Perhaps he was more worried about what we'd find than he would admit. He leaned forward. "If you're right, that could serve us well."

I let out a breath, relieved that it passed muster, even as the duplicity left a bitter taste in my mouth. How was it that revealing the truth required a twisting of it, in order to protect the innocent? Yet I'd made no direct claim the device was alchemical in nature—Stratesman Bancroft had made his own assumptions—and it did mark the seal of our bargain, thus repelling the fae. I tucked the imitation ward-stone away and sought to redirect the conversation. "How does Nelda fare?"

"She's quiet. Hasn't given trouble." Stratesman Bancroft frowned. "But even if her name's cleared, she has a difficult path ahead."

Unfortunately, he spoke truth, so I murmured something noncommittal and stared out at the passing forest, at the enormous trees thriving within, their ancient song thrumming deep and low, reaching for me.

I didn't dare lock the sensations away, lest I also block my ability to perceive the fae. I inhaled and closed my eyes. Only a bit longer, and I'd be done with all of this.

At last, we reached the mill. The ruined yard looked bleak indeed this morning. The water had receded, but the sinkhole remained a black abyss gaping before the water-stained cottage.

What must it be like for Melle to face such destruction? She didn't speak of it but emerged from her wagon in grim silence— and wordless, we walked down the path toward the weir bank. My hands slicked with the recollection of being drawn toward the depths by the merciless grip of the sprites. If I'd failed in crafting a bargain strong enough . . . no, I couldn't consider it. On leaden legs, I trudged behind Stratesman Bancroft, who watched our surroundings with a wary gaze.

Near the weir, the willows waved their branches in greeting, and beneath their boughs, the fae-circles gleamed, their cuplike plants glistening silver, as if the waters of the river had been distilled within their leaves.

Stratesman Bancroft kept a respectful distance, but he plucked a fallen branch and prodded at the nearest plant.

A faint mist emanated from its surface and spread tendrils toward us and toward the river simultaneously. And then they came, bound by their sworn word. The sinuous forms of the sprites broke the surface of the river, ripples spreading outward toward the shore.

Aunt Caris fluttered away, moaning a prayer.

Melle muttered imprecations.

Jade growled.

"Back, everyone!" Stratesman Bancroft shouted. He drew a dagger, as if it could provide defense.

Their leader lifted what looked like a tremendous spear fashioned of water. He flung it to shore, and where it landed, a tiny sinkhole appeared and began to spread.

Oh.

I'd wondered how they accomplished that.

Every line of Stratesman Bancroft's body tensed. "Miss Jessa, if your device offers any protection, you'd best use it now."

From the folds of my gown, I withdrew the ward-stone. Its gilded runes flashed in the early morning light, a flare of warm gold to oppose the cool silver of the waters. If I'd not known it was inert, I would have been impressed.

The water sprites halted, and the development of the sinkhole arrested. I stepped forward on trembling legs. "This marks the protection of the mill, of the weir, and of the river here. You must leave and never return."

The sprites remained motionless; perspiration trickled down my back. Their word bound them. We'd agreed upon this overt display. But had they found a loophole?

I gripped the ward-stone tighter.

Then the leader raised a fist, and they withdrew. Farther, farther. Almost faster than I could follow, their forms flashed away, up the river and beyond the weir, as they deported themselves to the home I'd promised them.

Oh, how I hoped it wasn't a bargain I'd come to regret. Legs trembling, I sank onto the bedewed grass and exhaled heavily. Jade glared at the river a moment longer through slitted eyes, then jumped into my lap.

Stratesman Bancroft scrubbed his face with his hands. "This is the last time I investigate a possible Otherkind sighting without sending for the Vigil first. Better to be taken for a fool than dead. If you'd not brought a ward-stone, Miss Jessa, we'd all have been in the bottom of the river, and no mistake."

Face pale, Aunt Caris gripped Melle's arm as if it were the only thing keeping her upright.

Melle simply stared at the river. "The miller here before . . . he drowned."

Stratesman Bancroft nodded. "Maybe they had a hand in that, but I suppose we'll never know for sure."

Then he waved toward the ward-stone. "Will that thing hold?"

"I have no reason to believe otherwise." For all lore held bargains with the fae unbreakable—*please, Infinite, may it be so.* "The mill should be safe now."

Melle pinned me with a sharp look. "I'll be staking the life of my family on it. You sure they're gone?"

"I'm certain."

"How is it you know so much, Miss Jessa?" Stratesman Bancroft asked.

"I told you, I spoke with Mr. Heard. He gave me so many warnings about the Otherkind, I wouldn't have dared venture here without some precaution." I kept my tone light, as if I was conversing with a gentleman over tea, as if my own fate didn't hang on easing any lingering suspicion. "I wanted to keep everyone safe if my fears proved correct. And if they were unfounded . . . well, I find the work of alchemists fascinating in its own right, so there would have been no great loss."

"In this case, great gain." Melle clapped her hands, looking years younger. "This will clear the miller's girl as well? I don't want her bearing a burden of a guilt that's not hers."

"It's evident she wasn't involved, at least not with this. So she'll be free to go, as long as she can keep herself from further trouble." Stratesman Bancroft tapped his fingers slowly against his leg.

Perhaps it was time to add a happier thought. I offered a brilliant smile. "I'm certain your superiors will be impressed that you've cleared up such a bewildering affair."

His eyes brightened. "Aye, they'll be well pleased. No one wants to muck around in the affairs of Milburn—not with the Crossing nearby. They'll be happy to have done with this, and no lives lost."

Melle offered polite thanks, and then Stratesman Bancroft announced he'd walk back to Milburn. His job managed, he had no interest in lingering to examine the house. When he vanished over the rise, a weight lifted from my shoulders.

Aunt Caris remained quiet, an abstracted expression on her face. At least she'd not questioned the ward-stone and how in the Crossings I'd procured it. My absence for the entire day yesterday gave some plausibility to the tale, but if she pressed, I couldn't invent a story, not for her.

I offered the ward-stone to Melle. "If you wish, you may keep this in the mill or the cottage, but I want to make sure I'm clear. Don't attempt to use it when dealing with other fae. Its . . . effectiveness is limited to this particular situation and these particular fae. It goes no further."

"Yes. Yes, I see." Melle nodded slowly. Then she took my

hand, an unexpected gesture given her usual brusqueness. "I'm grateful that after everything, you chose to take such a risk to help us."

"I could do no less." But I'd be ever so grateful to return to our townhome in Avons, to my familiar garden and the embrace of my family.

Together, we retraced our steps toward the cottage. Jade perched on my shoulders, her weight comforting, and the glow of answers and problems solved warmed me. Now that the burden of the future had lifted from Melle, I could ask the question weighing on my mind. I picked my way around a large patch of mud. "Melle, would you consider taking Nelda in, since she's not responsible for these attacks? She'd be another mouth to feed, but she's used to helping with the cottage and the mill. With her assistance, you could make repairs faster and—"

"Say no more." Melle bounded up the path, fresh energy in her steps. "I'll offer aid as I've been given it, so long as she's willing to join our household and share in the labors accordingly."

"Thank you." The cowslips along the way bobbed a cheery dance, and my heart lifted. With Nelda offered a home, I could return to Avons in peace. However much loss she'd suffered, she'd no longer be alone.

We skirted some puddles that lingered in the grassy yard and gave the sinkhole a wide berth. In time, they might fill it in—or at least fence it, so there would be no risk of another tumble.

Alongside Melle, we crossed the threshold of the cottage. While the structure remained sound, the interior had sustained damage. Muck and damp covered the floors and furniture and climbed several inches up the walls. Jade sneezed at the smell.

"Oh Melle, what will you do?" Aunt Caris asked, drawn from her thoughts at last.

"Work to reclaim it." Her jaw firmed. "I'm not afraid of labor, not when it brings the reward of home and haven for my family. But if I'd known Otherkind had laid claim to the mill . . ." She gusted out a sigh. "Well, what's past is done and gone, no matter how we might wish otherwise."

They would have a long journey ahead to repair the damages and make the mill profitable, not to mention change the views of influential townsfolk, but if determination and willingness to labor meant anything, they would succeed.

Melle disappeared down the hall and then returned with a small sheaf of letters, bound with red ribbon. "These belong to you."

Aunt Caris flicked a glance toward me as she reached for the letters.

For a moment longer than necessary, Melle held on to them also, until Aunt Caris met her gaze. "I'm sorry. More than you can ever know. For all this—and for all that you lost."

Aunt Caris tucked the sheaf into her reticule, then withdrew a bulging pouch of coins. "We shall let the past be past, as you say. But I'd like you to take this, to help repair the damage—a gift of friendship."

Melle stepped back. "I can't, not after—"

"You'll think of your family and accept. If it will make you feel better, consider it a loan. I might not have the funds to purchase a mill, but I have a small sum to use at my discretion."

"Fine, then." Melle swiped her hand across her eyes. "My thanks."

Aunt Caris drew her reticule shut, the letters inside rustling. She suddenly appeared weary, as though nothing remained to keep her upright. So I gently nudged her toward the door, and we took our leave.

Once inside the carriage, questions crowded my tongue,

demands that Aunt Caris confide about the mysterious letters and whatever secrets they contained. Melle had referred to a loss. Perhaps my notion of an improper love wasn't far off the mark. If she'd had to forsake him to please her family, it would certainly be a grievous loss—for if anyone was made to taste the joy of love, to be a wife and mother, it was Aunt Caris. But if she'd lost a love, how would Melle know of it? Their respective stations in life would not have lent themselves to easily forming such a close friendship, unless more lay hidden in Aunt Caris's past than I could begin to guess.

When I opened my mouth to inquire, she shook her head. A faint sheen of tears glistened in her eyes. "Don't ask, my dear. If you love me at all, let the past be the past."

I did. And so I would not press her, not now. After all, how could I condemn her, when I held secrets of my own, truths that threatened to choke the life from me?

I'd come out relatively unscathed from my dealings with the fae thus far. But my interactions with the Otherworld could just as easily have stolen my life, and still might steal my freedom, my future, and even my sanity. I stared out the window, the sprites' Otherwordly beauty dancing before my eyes—not an aberration, but a reality I could never escape. I shrank into myself, tugging my shawl closer around my shoulders.

As the miles rolled away, a misting rain fogged the carriage windows, obscuring my view and bathing our surroundings in a gentle haze. Even so, the soft songs of the flowers and trees murmured in my ears, a constant reminder of fae influence.

In this instance, the fae-touch had proven itself an asset— but what cost would its use exact? Had I hastened my inevitable descent into madness by permitting it liberty, however slight? I sought the gap within my cage of thorns, the breach in defenses that allowed a ceaseless flow of sensation. If such a small opening brought this onslaught, what would happen if my defenses eroded altogether? My skin pebbled, and I wrapped my arms across my chest but could not diminish the chill creeping over me.

The lively chirrups of the grasses by the roadside, the stolid songs of the gnarled oaks, and the healing scent of white-blossomed yarrow swirled around me, the sensations born of the Otherworld warm and welcoming. They invited me to surrender, to sink into their depths. I shook my head, attempting to clear it. However strong the allure, if I couldn't regain control, this influence would drown me. I would lose myself in the flood of Other and never surface again.

I rested my head against Jade, and she nestled close, her presence bringing calm, her warmth driving away the chill. No matter how much I might desire it, I could no longer lock away the fae-touch and pretend it didn't exist. It was part of me, undeniable as the sun rising and setting in its course. But nor could I accept that madness and Institutionalization were the only fates before me. If I were to have any hope of changing my future, I must gain understanding. Avons, with its capacious libraries and numerous loremasters, might offer avenues of exploration—and answers that could mean life or death to me.

Yet I would gain nothing if these sensations overtook me and caused me to inadvertently betray myself and bring down the wrath of the Vigil. For now, I must exercise control. Could I return this Otherwordly influence to its cage, until I gained greater understanding?

It was time to try.

I took one deep breath, then another. I could do this; I must. I imagined the vines growing within my mind once more, coiling together into a tight bundle, only this time the strands were larger, thicker, and more densely covered in thorns. I wove the vines tight and sealed the cage.

Pain seared my frame, as sudden and sharp as if I'd severed a limb. What was this? My vision faded, and I leaned into the carriage seat.

Jade pressed herself against me, *mrowing* low in my ear.

Breathe, just breathe.

An age passed before my sight cleared, before the pain ebbed. But at last, the world stopped spinning, and Aunt Caris came back into focus, a faint furrow lining her forehead.

"Are you well, my dear? You look dreadfully pale."

I sat up straighter, Jade wiggling from my grasp. "I'm well enough, only weary."

"And no wonder. When I think of you bargaining with those dreadful creatures—" She squeezed my hand. "Thank the Infinite it ended without harm."

"Indeed." I choked out the word, smothering the desire to rest my head on her shoulder and pour out my fears, my sorrow, my shame. Instead, I closed my eyes, blotting out her concern. "I think I'll rest a bit."

She murmured her agreement and fussed about me, covering me with one of her shawls in addition to my own. What would she say if she knew? It would place her in an impossible predicament: bound by law to turn me over to the Vigil, bound by love to protect me.

No, what happened in Milburn would stay here, for my safety and that of my family. The only debt I owed was a visit to Mr. Heard to confide as little as possible of the events of today. After that, Avons and answers . . . or so I hoped.

In order to protect my family and our futures, my fae-touch must stay hidden. But whatever the cost, I'd figure out how it had come upon me. And were it possible, I'd learn to govern this influence before it ruled me, body and soul. This taint might need to remain concealed from the rest of the world, but I'd no longer run from it. I would chase the truth—however dangerous it might prove.

It was time to unearth secrets.

EPILOGUE

One more night spent away from home, in a quiet inn called The Avesby, and then I would return to the safety of the familiar. As we traveled day after day, I'd bent my thoughts on it, dreaming of immersing myself in my sketchbooks and herbalism, of sorting Father's correspondence, of assisting Ibbie with her antiquarian works and listening to her no-nonsense lectures. Surely those familiar acts would help bring peace while I sought the answers I needed and strengthen my endeavors to manage the fae-touch, which still battered relentlessly at the fraying cage of vines within.

A quiet rap sounded at the door of our sitting room, and a maid brought in a tray laden with tea and scones, accompanied by creamy butter and a rich citrus marmalade. I poured out steaming cups of lavender tea for Aunt Caris and myself, inhaling the soothing aroma.

Aunt Caris, seated across the small table, absently accepted the cup as she examined a gazette.

Abruptly, her grip on the page tightened, crumpling the edges. "Oh heavens. How can it be?"

"What is it, Aunt Caris?"

She closed her eyes and moaned. "Just think of your sweet sisters alone in Avons—they must be so afraid. And goodness knows it never occurs to your father to offer comfort."

Afraid? The flaky scone became dry as dust in my mouth. "What's happened?"

"Read for yourself, dear." She offered me the gazette, her soft features drawn tight.

I unfolded the rumpled pages and read:

Brutal murder!
Evil stalks Avons

Last night, the ruthless murderer dubbed the *Crimson Tattoo Killer* claimed his fifth known victim, a housekeeper of good character and long service in the townhome of Lord Barclay. No one witnessed the murder, and the killer left no evidence. The Magistry continues to investigate, despite the lack of leads.

The stratesman in charge refuses to discuss the condition in which the body was found, saying only that it was a violent death.

Prior to the housekeeper, four others fell victim to this brutality: an elderly solicitor, a sailor of the *Eventide*, a paper boy, and a lady of the night, all strangers to each other. Such a spate of vicious death must surely be the work of a lunatic. If so, no one in our great city is safe.

An anonymous source confirmed the housekeeper bore the same tattoo of crimson that the other victims received before their deaths. None recalled receiving the tattoo, but after discovering the mark, all died within a fortnight. This latest ghastly murder occurred only three days after the tattoo appeared. The housekeeper confided its appearance in no one save her sister; if she had gone to the authorities, perhaps her life might have been saved.

The column continued on the next page, but for a moment the black letters blurred to gray against the stark white page. I read on, my head spinning. Three murders had occurred before we left for Milburn but had been kept hidden. And now two more since our departure? So many violent deaths in such a short time seemed impossible for our peaceful city.

Surely our family remained well, for we'd had no word otherwise. But for how long? What would we find upon our return? It seemed that Avons did not intend to offer safe haven after all.

AFTERWORD

Want to find out what Jessa reported to Mr. Heard about the sprites? **Get the free bonus scene.**

go.sarahchislon.com/witw-bonus

Jessa's adventures continue in *Tattoo of Crimson*! **You can pre-order today.**

go.sarahchislon.com/toc-preorder

ACKNOWLEDGMENTS

It's an absolute delight to craft stories and a joy to share them—but there's also a great deal of work involved, and I'm deeply grateful for those who have helped me along the way. Through my journey as a writer, my biggest supporter and champion has been my wonderful husband—he's my first beta reader and foremost encourager. CJ, thank you for your endless enthusiasm for my books and for the countless ways you've offered support. I love you now and always!

I'm also very thankful for the other beta reader input I've received—August Head, your in-depth commentary was particularly helpful.

In addition, I've had the privilege of working with two fantastic editors: Lauren Donovan and Kara Aisenbrey. Lauren and Kara, your astute insights and thoughtful feedback made this book stronger, and your enthusiasm for the story provided tremendous encouragement. I couldn't have asked for better editors! Thanks also to Emily Poole for lending her keen editorial eye for the final proofread.

To my sweet daughters who love stories and take delight in having a mama who writes books—your joy and creativity provide constant inspiration. I'm forever thankful for you!

To my family and friends who have encouraged me along my writing and publishing journey, I greatly appreciate you.

And most of all, I thank God for His work of grace in my life and for the privilege of creating with Him.

ABOUT THE AUTHOR

Sarah Chislon lives in Virginia with her husband and three daughters. When she's not writing, she's homeschooling her children and running a web development business with her husband. As an avid reader and a lifelong story-weaver, she delights in creating fantastic worlds and exploring them alongside her characters.

For more information on her books, visit her website sarahchislon.com—or sign up for her newsletter to receive updates and free bonus content.